WHY WON'T MY BOOBS GROW...
AND OTHER ANNOYANCES

To Nancy —
I couldn't have done
this without you!

[signature]

this without you!

[signature]

WHY WON'T MY BOOBS GROW... AND OTHER ANNOYANCES

Rebecca Garner

NEW DEGREE PRESS

WHY WON'T MY BOOBS GROW... AND OTHER ANNOYANCES

ISBN

979-8-88504-914-6   *Paperback*

979-8-88504-766-1   *Kindle Ebook*

979-8-88504-245-1   *Digital Ebook*

For thirteen-year-old Bex. (They grew!)

And for the teenage girls out there like her and Emma.

I see you.

Contents

Author's Note

Do you remember what it was like to be thirteen? No, really, think about it. When you're thirteen, every time something good happens, it's the best day of your life; when something bad happens, your life is basically over. Having a good hair day and wearing a cute new outfit? Watch out, world. I can do anything! A zit pops up on the day of your big presentation? Goodbye forever. I live in my bedroom now.

I remember being thirteen so vividly. I was a frizzy-haired, flat-chested brace-face. I flushed when I was in the same room with a boy I liked. I was afraid I didn't know how to kiss. I was your average thirteen-year-old girl. No magical powers (despite all my wishing). No wild adventures. No heroics.

And all I wanted was to be seen and loved.

After I grew up, I taught middle school. When I would tell people this, they'd gasp, "Why? They're horrible." And yeah, sometimes they are.

But they're also so full of emotion, passion, and confusion, and they don't know how to deal with it yet. They're trying to figure out how to process and express these feelings and ideas and grow into themselves, into the adults who'll one day gasp at the idea of spending all day with them.

I knew that was where my heart was.

When I decided I was actually going to write this book, Emma started spilling onto the page very easily (at least at the beginning) because so much of Emma is based on me and my experiences as a teenage girl. I was convinced I would be a cool adult (with boobs) who would always remember what it was like to be this age. "I'll remember how important it is to be able to go to the bathroom and check on your hair," or "I'll remember how real this love is," or "I'll remember how important your friends are." I guess I was right about two of the three. (Boobs? Check. Remembering? Check. Cool? You can't check all the boxes ...)

This book peeks underneath that surface-level moody teenager and shows what it's like inside their brain. When you're too old to be a kid but too young to be an adult, floating around somewhere in between.

This book is for those girls who, like I was, are your average teenagers. Who are trying to figure out who they are, who to trust, and what's important to them. I want readers to see themselves in Emma and realize that, even if their lives are ordinary, that doesn't mean they're not extraordinary.

But it's not only for teenage girls. Have you ever wished you could change your appearance? Have you ever had an all-consuming crush? Have you ever had a fight with a friend? Then this book is for you. I hope it reminds you what it was like to be a teenager—the drama, the heartache, the silliness.

It's a coming-of-age story with a side of laughter. There's a massive zit, bad kissing, and shouting, "Penis!" There's also teenage love, friendship, moments of self-reflection, and courage.

Emma is just starting to figure out who she is. I can't wait for you to join her.

CHAPTER 1

It's so big it's practically pulsing.

THURSDAY, APRIL 22ND
7:06 A.M.

I have a massive zit on my face. I *cannot* handle this today. I put my head in my hands. Not that I handle zits very well any day, but today especially. (Also, why doesn't everyone use "zit"? The word "pimple" really grosses me out.)

My presentation is today! We had to write argumentative essays for Ms. Stein's English class this quarter. I wrote mine about why cats make the ideal pet. I'm actually pretty proud of it. I spent a lot of time choosing exactly the right gifs and pictures of kittens. But that doesn't mean I want to stand in front of the class, looking like Rudolph, and share it.

Uuuggghhh! Why can't we do the work, turn it in, and move on? I swear, the teachers gather in their lunchroom and plot ways to make us miserable. I can just imagine them cackling over their lunches—probably tuna sandwiches or something equally as disgusting.

I look in the mirror again. The zit is sitting on the bridge of my nose. It's so big it's practically pulsing, like a big, red mountain. It hurts just to look at it. What am I going to do? I can't go out in public like this. Maybe Mom will let me stay home today...

Cough Yeah, *cough.* I'm suddenly feeling like poop...

I throw myself back into my bed and roll onto my side so I can stare at the beautiful faces of the band Celsius. I hug my stuffed piggy tightly and gently breathe in his comforting scent.

7:28 A.M.

Where is Mom? Why hasn't she come in to check on me yet? I'm bored...

7:30 A.M.

Albus saunters in and hops up on the bed with me.

"Good morning, handsome boy." I try to pet his adorable gray head. He responds with a swat on my nose.

"Seriously? It's bad enough there as it is." I cautiously touch my nose. Yep, still there. His black pupils stare at me unblinkingly. Then he turns and lifts a leg straight up in the air, so he can lick his butt. "Thanks for your support." Still licking. "Can you do that somewhere else, please?" I know cats need to clean themselves, but does he have to do it in such a showy way?

7:34 A.M.
STILL IN BED

Mom finally comes into my room. "Emma! Why aren't you dressed yet?" She pushes on my shoulder, and I fake groggily turn over. At first, all I see is blue fuzz, but then I realize my mother is standing there in a towel. Gross. What if it falls off? I'll be scarred forever.

"Ew, Mom!" I start to shout, but then I remember I'm supposed to be sick. I lower my head back onto my pillow delicately and try to hide my outburst with a cough. "Ugh... Mommy," I whine. I scrunch up my face in a way I imagine makes me look like I am very ill. "I don't feel good." I rub my forehead for good measure.

"Oh, *Mommy*, huh?" She raises her eyebrows skeptically at me. "Does this have anything to do with that pimple on your nose?"

"I don't know what you're talking about." I pull my covers up over my face. "And can you please not use the word *pimple*? It's disgusting."

"You're going to school," she says with a finality that tells me not to bother arguing. "And you better hurry up. We're leaving in twenty minutes. You won't have time to walk today." She pauses at the door, looking back at me. "I can help you cover that up if you want."

"No!" I shout, still hiding under my covers.

As soon as the door closes, I fly out of bed. I look in the mirror. *Oh, crap.* Not only do I have my new friend on my nose, but my hair is standing up in every direction. I find my brush halfway hidden underneath the magazines and notebooks on my desk and try to smooth it out in the back. *That's what you get for not showering in the morning,* I can hear my friend Cher saying with her usual superior-ness. I sigh and walk over to my dresser, pulling open the top drawer. I grab my padded training bra out of its special place. I'm going to need all the help I can get today.

7:53 A.M.
IN THE CAR

By some sort of miracle, I am ready and waiting in the car within the twenty minutes Mom gave me. However, in the usual fashion, my mother and my *endearing* little sister are not. I reach over and honk the horn three times. While I wait, I check my appearance in the mirror. I think I did a decent job covering up my zit. I can barely see its red head, waiting to poke out from underneath Mom's cover-up. I had to use hers for this heavy-duty task. My five-dollar Covergirl wasn't going to cut it today.

7:58 A.M.
They are still not outside. I honk the horn again.

7:59 A.M.
Still nothing. I ram my fist onto the horn, but I don't lift it off this time. The horn blares.

8:00 A.M.
My sister, Marie, comes strolling out of the house like she has all the time in the world. She's nine, but she tries to act like she's twenty-five. Mom must have been doing her hair. It's pulled up into two little buns on either side of her head.

"Geez, calm down," Marie says, poking her buns in the window. "It's my turn to ride in front."

"I was here first." I lock the door.

"Whatever." She stares at me with her round brown eyes as she pauses to touch her buns. Then she lets out with a burst of energy, "At least I don't have a big zit on my nose."

"Oh my God! Shut up!" I try to reach out of the car to smack her arm. She jumps out of my way and scurries into the back seat.

"Seriously? How can you two be fighting already?" Mom shouts as she tries to shut the front door without Albus escaping. She fails. I unbuckle my seat belt and start to open the car door to go grab him. "No," she says. "He'll be fine for the day. Berniece will snag him."

I close my door, but only because I don't want to be late for school. "He always has really bad farts after Berniece feeds him," I moan.

Berniece is our neighbor. If her name didn't give it away, she's an old lady, and she loves Albus. Whenever he gets locked out of the house, he'll wander over by her. She gives him these small, stringy treats—like string cheese for cats, kind of. He loves them, but I'm the one who has to smell his farts all night long.

Mom ignores me. I reach up and pull down the visor mirror to check on my zit. Yep, still there. I flip the visor up with more force than I probably need to and lean my head back against the seat with a huff.

CHAPTER 2

There is something massive on your nose.

THURSDAY, APRIL 22ND
8:06 A.M.
SCHOOL DROP-OFF

"Okay, bye!" I yell as I close the door. I tentatively touch the bridge of my nose before I start walking. Some powder lingers on the tip of my finger. Better stop touching. Marie struggles with her backpack behind me, and I hesitate as she fixes it. I wipe my sweaty hands on my blue plaid skirt, and I start toward school.

I'm trying to play it cool and not look rushed as I speed walk to the entrance. We go to a small, private school, so Marie and I are in the same building even though we're four grades apart.

I see Ruby and Cher standing off to the side, and I casually sprint over to them. My two best friends couldn't look more different. Cher is the shortest of the three of us with ivory skin, blond hair, and green eyes while Ruby's brown skin is complemented by her dark brown eyes and long braids. Ruby and Cher have one thing in common, though. They both have boobs. I'm the outlier there.

"Hi," I say breathlessly.

"Hi, Em," says Ruby, reaching her arm out to give me a quick hug.

"What is that?" I ask, pointing to the bulky bag in her hand.

"Oh, it's for my presentation." Ruby smiles. Of course, she does; Ruby has no problem being the center of attention. She doesn't seek it out, but it's no big deal to her. She doesn't get nervous because she's so easily herself all the time. She doesn't care what anyone else thinks about what she's doing or saying; if it makes her happy, that's enough for her. If only I could be more like that.

Cher rolls her eyes. "It's a bunch of kiddie instruments." She smooths a nonexistent wrinkle on her skirt. This reminds me to roll my skirt up a little. Mom won't have it hemmed, so it's almost down past my knees. Cher's is actually cute, hitting a little above her knee. On the other hand, mine is like a nun's uniform, which was probably the intention behind the uniforms in the first place.

"Why?" I try to peek into her bag as I fiddle with the waist of my skirt.

She shifts the bag in her hand so I can look inside. I see a xylophone, a tambourine, a little guitar, and a recorder like the ones we had to play in music last year. "I wrote about the importance of music education, and I thought a demonstration would really help prove my argument."

"That's creative," I tell her.

"Sure," Cher says, turning to me. "What's happening here?" She waves her hand over my face.

I feel my cheeks getting warm. "What do you mean?" I glance at Ruby. Her big brown eyes look quickly away.

"There is something massive on your nose." She wrinkles her own nose as if mine has offended her.

"Nothing." I decide to pretend I don't know what she's talking about.

"Whatever you say." Cher grabs her backpack from the ground as the bell rings for us to go in. I turn to Ruby.

"It's fine," she reassures me. "I didn't even notice."

"Liar." I hip-bump her as we walk in. "Do you think Connor will notice?"

"Do boys even notice things like that?" she asks. Easy for her to say. I've literally never seen a zit on her smooth brown skin.

"For my sake, let's hope not," I groan.

8:15 A.M.
HALLWAY

"So." Cher closes her locker, which is right next to mine. "You ready for your presentation today?" She raises her perfect eyebrows at me.

Cher transferred to St. Lucy's halfway through last year. On her first day, she was sitting alone at lunch, so Ruby and I invited her to sit with us. I think people were intimidated by her. She constantly looks like she's irritated, but that's just her face. And even though we wear uniforms, Cher always stands out with her perfect makeup and expensive-looking jewelry. I'm not even allowed to wear any makeup to school, except cover-up on these stupid zits when I get them.

"As I'll ever be," I tell Cher. "I think my project is good, but I'm so nervous about getting up in front of everybody, you know?"

Cher shrugs. "Not really."

I don't know how I ended up with two best friends who are so confident. Then there's me, avoiding being the center of attention at all costs.

As we walk toward English, Cher says about Connor?"

"Of course I am. You know that." Conn and cool. He's the pitcher on the baseball tea runner on the track team. His skin is a golden has wavy dark brown hair with piercing blue eyes. I. dreamboat, as my mom would say.

There's no way he's interested in me. He likes confident, pretty girls like Cher or Ruby. Not easily embarrassed, flat-chested girls like me.

"I'm going to stop in the bathroom real quick," I tell Cher. "I'll see you in class."

She waves and keeps walking.

8:18 A.M.
BATHROOM

I examine my nose in the mirror. I can definitely see the zit. The pit of dread already in my stomach sinks further. I take Mom's makeup out of my skirt pocket and dab on some more. Then I try to maneuver some pieces of hair to cover the crease in the back. I really need to stop showering at night.

I take in my appearance one more time. My green eyes stare back at me. I swear I can still see the zit, despite reapplying the makeup. I run my fingers through my slightly wavy brown hair and push it back behind my ears. At least that's a little better.

I scurry out of the bathroom and across the hall to class.

8:23 A.M.
ENGLISH

After morning announcements, our teacher, Ms. Stein, claps her hands together. "Who's ready for their presentation?" No one responds. A couple of people groan, most noticeably

Hunter. He's a big lug. He never does his work, so I don't know why he's groaning. He probably won't even present.

Ms. Stein ignores the groans and continues, "You have had plenty of time to prepare. Two days a week in class for the last five weeks, plus your own time at home. I have high expectations for these projects." She scans the room, lingering on Hunter, who smiles in a pained way.

"Who wants to go first?" she asks. Both Ruby and Cher shoot their hands up into the air. I slide further down in my seat. Maybe if I hide like this, she'll forget all about me...

9:03 A.M.
STILL ENGLISH

"Who's next?" Ms. Stein asks from her grading station at the front of the class. The few people who wanted to volunteer have already gone, so no hands are in the air. She turns around in her seat, eying us with one eyebrow raised. How do people do that? As I'm trying to hide, I also try to imitate her one-eyebrow lift.

I think I'm nailing it when my concentration is broken by Ms. Stein's scratchy voice. "Emma? Does that face mean you want to go next?"

Oh, God. Oh, God. No. No, it doesn't. "Oh, um... no... do I have to?" I can feel everyone's eyes on me. I sneak a peek toward Connor, who sits a few rows over. Even *he* is looking at me. My cheeks start to burn.

"Yes." She writes something down on the rubric in front of her. "Go get yourself set up."

I sit in my seat for another couple of seconds, hoping she'll forget. Instead, Ms. Stein starts rambling on again about being respectful to our peers during the presentations. "Remember, it's hard to get up in front of our classmates. We are a *community*. We *support* each other."

Alejandra, the girl who sits behind me, pokes me in the back. "Go," she whispers. I turn around and give her the evil eye. She pokes me again. So much for *supporting* me. I drag myself out of my seat and make my way up to the front of the room, my heart pounding inside my chest and my cheeks warming with every second that passes.

I turn to face the class, and my stomach does a loop de loop. I shuffle through my notecards, quadruple-checking that they're in order.

Ms. Stein clicks her pen. "Whenever you're ready, Emma."

I force myself to look up from the notecards. Ms. Stein gives me an encouraging smile. I swallow the lump in my throat and start. "Seventy percent of families in the US have pets..."

"Awwww," a few people say as I move on to my next slide. They are loving my kitten gifs. This isn't so bad. I feel like I'm kind of on a roll. Feeling emboldened by the "Aw," I look around the room a bit.

Something turns over in my stomach when I see Audrey, who has a forehead the size of a football field, yet always has a boyfriend. She's watching me very intently. At first, it gives me a little more confidence, and I smile as I continue my presentation.

I glance at Audrey again, and she's still staring at me. Very slowly, she brings her hand up to her nose and scratches it. Right on the bridge. My confidence wavers a bit. Her eye contact is freaking me out. I shift my gaze to Ruby, and she gives me a smile and a thumbs-up.

It's fine. Everything is fine. Audrey's just trying to throw me off.

Then Hunter catches my attention in the front row. Now he is scratching the bridge of his nose. Instinctively, I touch my own, and that's when I remember the zit. Heat creeps up my neck. Oh, God. Why is this happening to me?

I try to shake off the overwhelming embarrassment boiling up inside of me and continue on with my presentation. I'm almost done. I'm at my counterargument and rebuttal (dogs need training and walks and cost a lot more, and pets like lizards are creepy and don't offer any companionship). I turn toward the other side of the room and see Zoe, Audrey's best friend and follower, scratching her nose. I look down at my note cards. I chance another peek at the audience as I go into my snake example, and all I can see are people scratching their noses.

It's happening everywhere, and they're all doing it the same with one finger, slowly scratching the bridge of their nose. My whole face feels like it's on fire. My eyes start to sting. My voice wavers. My eyes find Cher; her forehead is creased with confusion.

Oh, no. It's going to happen. When I feel the first tear escape, I vow not to look up again, no matter what it does to my grade. I try to keep my voice steady as I say, "If you need more proof that cats make the ideal pet, watch this video of my cat, Albus, standing up like a bear."

I play the video, staring straight down at my note cards. When it ends, I mumble, "Thank you," and walk directly back to my seat, my eyes glued to the floor.

"That was really good up until the end," Alejandra whispers.

I put my head down on my arms as Ms. Stein asks for the next victim.

CHAPTER 3

Forget them!

THURSDAY, APRIL 22ND
12:06 P.M.
LUNCH

"Well, that could not have gone worse," I say to Cher and Ruby at lunch. I bang my head against the table.

"That's not true," Ruby says, rubbing my back. I peek up at her and then at Cher.

Cher sighs. "She's right, Emma. It really wasn't *that* bad."

"But that also means it wasn't good." I moan and put my head back on the table.

"Emma, it's okay. Not everyone was doing it," Ruby says. She shakes my arm gently.

With that, I have a sudden realization. I lift my head up slowly. "Guys..."

Cher and Ruby both wait for me to say something. When I continue to stare at them silently, Ruby says, "Yeeesss?" dragging the word out.

I shake my head slightly in an attempt to jostle my memory. "I... I don't think Connor did it."

"Are you sure?" Cher asks tentatively. Her eyebrows are raised slightly.

"I think I would remember if *Connor* was doing it," I retort. My heart starts to feel a little lighter.

Ruby nods enthusiastically. "Totally." She pauses for a second. "Ooh! Maybe he likes you," she says, bouncing up and down in her seat.

I don't even know what to say. Could he actually like me? I mean, even Hunter, who is his best friend, was part of the nose scratching. Why wouldn't he join in? I let a small smile creep onto my face for the first time since English.

Cher snorts. "Or he didn't know about it."

"Okay, harsh, Cher," Ruby says.

My cheeks flush, and my heart sinks back down into the depths of my chest. Of course, Connor doesn't like me. Why would he? Look at my nose. Without thinking, I gingerly touch it. Cher narrows her eyes slightly, and I pull my hand away from the monster.

"Ugh. Emma, you're too sensitive," Cher snaps. "Maybe you need to be a little more realistic about what's going on around you. Both of you."

Ruby rolls her eyes and takes a bite of her applesauce, and I stare down at my sandwich, not really hungry.

Cher sighs. "I'm just trying to be honest." She pushes a piece of blond hair behind her ear. A little more gently, she says, "I don't want you to get your hopes up about something that isn't going to happen, Em."

I continue staring at my sandwich, my cheeks still warm. Ruby gently kicks me under the table.

"I'm trying to be a good friend," Cher says finally.

I force a smile. "Mmhm. I know you are," I say as normally as I can. Even though I don't think Connor likes me, it still hurts when someone else says it. Even if they're *just trying to be honest.* And why is Cher so convinced that Connor couldn't like me? Am I so horrible that she can't even imagine it? Sure, we basically never talk, but on the other hand, he definitely wasn't scratching his nose today.

12:23 P.M.
BATHROOM

"Is it really that noticeable?" I ask Ruby and Cher. The three of us are gathered around the mirror. All I can see is the red mountain pulsing under the cover-up on my face.

"I tried to ask you about it this morning." Leave it to Cher to be brutally honest, again. My eyes start to sting.

Ruby gives me a hug. "Everyone gets them, Em."

"She's right," Cher says, joining the hug.

Through my sniffles, I say, "But everyone was doing it." After that, nothing I say is understandable, even to me.

"Forget them! People can be so rude!" Ruby is starting to get angry. Uh-oh. She puts her hands on either side of my face, so I'm looking directly at her. Her brown eyes bore into my green ones. "Emma. You are awesome. Forget the presentation. Forget stupid Audrey and stupid Zoe. Forget anyone who doesn't make you feel like you are awesome. Because you are." She lets go of my face. "Awesome." She pokes me in the chest to emphasize her point.

"You said awesome like sixty times in that sentence," Cher says, exasperated.

I rub the spot where Ruby poked me. It hurts a little.

"Words are not my strength," Ruby responds, swirling her pointer finger in the air. I giggle. She crosses her eyes and sticks out her tongue. I giggle some more.

"Yes, that's it," Ruby says. "Let it out, Emma." She stomps her foot.

"Forget them!" I shout, jumping up and punctuating with my pointer finger in the air. "Forget them! Forget them!" Ruby and I jump up and down, chanting, "Forget them!"

Cher takes her phone out of her pocket and takes a picture of us. "You two are weirdos." We pause our chanting to look at her with disbelief. "But *awesome* ones," she adds as she comes hopping over.

"Forget them!" She starts the chant back up. We link up in a circle, jumping and chanting until Mrs. Short, our science teacher, comes in the bathroom.

"What is going on in here?" she demands. "I can hear you out in the hallway."

"Nothing," we all say at once, breaking from our circle.

"Just using the washroom before class, Mrs. Short," Cher says sweetly. She grabs her books from the floor. "We better get going. The bell is going to ring soon."

Ruby and I follow suit. I smile meekly, and Ruby waves as we walk past Mrs. Short. She follows us out and watches us walk down the hallway. When we're finally out of her sight, Ruby jumps in the air and subsequently drops her books.

"Oh, poo." She fumbles around, trying to grab everything.

"Forget them!" I say in a high-pitched, mouse voice. We burst into a fit of laughter as the bell rings.

2:21 P.M.
HOMEROOM

"I have some exciting news," Ms. Stein, who doubles as both our English teacher and homeroom, announces. "We are going on a field trip next month."

Everyone cheers. Cher silently claps her hands, and Ruby does a little jig in her seat. Ms. Stein starts handing out letters and permission slips. I tune out what she's saying, in anticipation of reading the letter. I finally get my hands on one: *The eighth-grade students will attend "The Human Reproductive System" at the Center for Health Education.*

What? Is this a joke? This is not a field trip. It's a class. I tune back in to Ms. Stein's commentary. "As you know, we don't have a health class that meets state requirements, so this will be a supplement to our *Family Life* lessons." She pauses, looking around the room. "There will be discussions of some sensitive topics, including puberty and reproduction. You will be separated by gender. Boys will attend a presentation with a male presenter, and ladies will attend a presentation with a female presenter." She smiles. "Any questions?"

We are going on a "field trip" to talk about periods and sex. Oh my God. I look over at Ruby. She's leaning forward onto her desk, staring back at me wide-eyed. I turn, and two rows behind Ruby, Cher has a subtle smirk on her face, but she won't make eye contact.

As if this day couldn't get worse. Why are we even doing this? Most of the girls in our class already have their period. At least I think they do. Cher does, and so does Ruby. Ruby called me screaming when hers came over the summer before seventh grade, and she refused to even be near a pool for two weeks. Laney Lindt got hers in fifth grade. And everyone knows Jillian Elam has hers because she does a horrible job of hiding her pads in her pocket. I might be the only one who doesn't have it yet.

That's right. I haven't gotten my period. I get giant zits on my face, but I have no boobs, and I don't get to carry around tampons in my purse. Although, I'm terrified of tampons—what if one gets stuck up there? Maybe they'll talk about that on our "field trip."

I glance around the room. Everyone is talking to their neighbors, either rolling their eyes or giggling about the field trip. My eyes dart to Connor. He's looking over his shoulder in my direction. My heart jolts to a stop. He's not *looking in my direction*. He's looking *at* me. He turns back to say something to Hunter so quickly, though, I think maybe I imagined it.

CHAPTER 4

My sister scratched her nose at me.

I hear Marie opening and closing cabinets in the kitchen. "I'm hungry," she whines.

"Then eat something," I snap from my position on the couch.

"Make something for me." She stands in the doorway with her hands on her hips.

"No."

"Yes!"

"Um, no." Albus hops up on the couch with me. I pet him as he settles down into a ball on my belly. Then he lets a nasty fart rip. "Oh my God, Albus! Get off me!" I push him, and he leaps off the couch and onto the chair across the room. He curls up into a little ball again and settles his gaze on me. "Don't look at me like that," I tell him. "You're the one whose butthole smells like rotten eggs."

I roll off the couch and walk toward the sound of slamming cabinets. "When did Mom say she'll be home?"

"I don't know." Marie sits down at the table and looks at me expectantly. "What are you going to make me?"

"Nothing." I grab a bag of Cheetos and throw them at her. I sit in the chair across from her with my Cool Ranch Doritos.

She sighs but opens the bag. She eats one and then looks up at me and scratches her nose.

"What is your problem?" I shout at her, standing up. I feel so angry that my vision blurs for a second. It was bad enough when everyone was making fun of my monster zit at school. Now I have to deal with it at home, too?

"Whoa, calm down." The excitement on Marie's face immediately fades. "I didn't think you'd get so mad."

"Why did you do that?" I sit back down.

"I don't know. I thought it would be funny. I heard you and Ruby talking about it on the way home."

I narrow my eyes at her. "Well, it's not funny. It was something really mean that happened to me today."

"What was it?" Marie shoves a handful of Cheetos into her mouth.

"I don't want to talk about it." I look down at my bag of chips. I'm suddenly not hungry anymore. "I'm going upstairs to do my homework. Leave me alone until Mom gets home. Okay?"

"Okay." She shrugs. "Thanks for the snack."

3:35 P.M.
BEDROOM

I sit down at my desk/makeshift vanity. It's super old, but Dad painted it white to match the mirror I have leaning up against the wall. It contrasts nicely with my lavender room. I didn't make my bed this morning. I didn't have enough time. My covers are all rumpled, and my stuffed pig, Piggy, is standing on his head in the corner. I wish I'd stayed in bed with him all day.

The sun is shining through the window next to my bed, and for no reason at all, it annoys me. I let out a long sigh and grab my phone to text Ruby and Cher.

Me: My sister scratched her nose at me.

Ruby: Oh, no, really?

Cher: How did she know?

Me: She heard Ruby and me talking about it on our walk home.

Cher: She's a brat.

Me: Only I can say that, Cher.

Cher sends back the eye-roll emoji.

Ruby: I'm sorry all that happened, Emma.

Me: It's just so embarrassing.

Cher: Definitely.

Ruby: Everyone will forget about it in a few days. Forget them! Remember?

Me: Yeah…

I turn the screen off and throw my phone onto the bed.

I've been staring at the same math problem for at least five minutes, but my brain isn't working. Why bother? I turn on some music and lie on my bed, staring at the ceiling.

My thoughts immediately go to Connor. He definitely wasn't scratching his nose today, but he had to know about it. Right? I'm alone, but I blush anyway. And if he knew about the nose scratching, he definitely saw the zit. My cheeks warm another ten degrees, and I feel a lump in the back of my throat.

I like him *so* much, and I've liked him *forever*. We could be such a cute couple. We could walk home together. I could go to his baseball games and bring him Gatorade. We could hang out at his house and watch TV, and his mom would think we're so cute. And he could text me every night before bed and every morning when he wakes up...

Audrey butts her way into my thoughts, interrupting my pleasant daydream. I'm not sure if Connor likes her or if he only puts up with her, but she definitely likes him. She's always staring at him, asking him to do things for her, and laughing at what he says. Somehow, she sits near him in every single class. And Audrey's pretty much perfect, too. She's tall with long, blond hair and blue eyes, and her uniform is short enough to be cute but long enough that it's not breaking the dress code. If the rumors are true, she doesn't wear shorts underneath her skirt, either. Plus, like everyone except me, she has boobs. But ugh, she's horrible! And not only to me, either.

A couple months ago, she stole Laney Lindt's journal and posted pictures of it. Laney had written that she wished the anime characters she loved were real. Audrey's comment on the picture said *Oh. My. God. How old are we? #freak*. Laney was so embarrassed that she didn't come to school for the rest of the week. I felt bad for her. I mean, yeah, she's a little weird and doesn't really talk to anyone. But that doesn't mean Audrey can go through her stuff and share it with the world. When Laney came back to school on Monday, Ruby went up to her and gave her a hug. "Audrey is the worst," she told Laney. Laney was a little shocked but nodded and said thanks before shuffling off to class.

And now this nose-scratching business. I have enough to worry about without Audrey pointing out my every ugliness.

I wish I was brave enough to confront her. I picture it in my head. I walk up to her in the hallway. "Audrey," I say in a tone that demands respect. "What you did yesterday was not okay." Her eyes widen, and she takes a step back. I take another step forward. "Stop being such a bully. No one is perfect." I pause for dramatic effect. "Especially you." I turn and walk the opposite way down the hall. People are clapping and cheering me on.

CHAPTER 5

I'm fine.

THURSDAY, APRIL 22ND
4:28 P.M.

Mom's home. I hear her drop her keys in the dish by the door
and say something to Marie. I stay in my room, feeling sorry
for myself. And Laney Lindt.

4:49 P.M.

I hear Dad walk in. I continue staring at the ceiling in
my bedroom.

4:52 P.M.

Mom knocks on the door. "Come in," I tell her. There's no
keeping her out anyway. I once put a sign on my door that
said no one over the age of eighteen was allowed in, but she
flat out ignored it.

"Dinner will be ready in about half an hour." She frowns
a little. "What are you doing? Why are you lying there like
that? You look like a vampire."

"Nothing." I sit up. "Doing homework." I walk over and sit
back down at my desk.

"Okay…" she says, but she lingers in the doorway.

"I'm fine," I tell her. "But I'm hungry. Go make dinner."

"Okay." She puts her hands up in surrender and heads back downstairs.

5:30 P.M.
DINNER

"How did your presentation go today, Emma?" Mom asks as she passes Dad the corn.

"Was that the one about cats?" Dad asks, taking a big spoonful.

I nod. "You have something in your mustache."

He licks it. "Mmmmm, corn cream. I was saving it."

"Gross," I say, but I giggle despite myself.

Mom continues pestering me. "So, how did it go?"

Why must they know everything?

"Fine." I scoop a bite of mashed potatoes into my mouth so I don't have to talk anymore. I start coughing. *Too much. Too much!*

"Drink some water," Mom tells me although she doesn't seem too concerned about the fact that I'm choking.

"Let's play High-Low," Marie suggests. High-Low is a game we play at dinner some nights. We each go around and say a High (the best part of our day) and a Low (the worst part of our day). "I'll start," she volunteers. She looks around to make sure we're all listening. "High: I finally perfected my symbol." She smiles and raises her eyebrows. "You may have seen it when you came in. I drew it on the sidewalk."

"That's great, baby," Mom says. Dad gives her a high-five. I roll my eyes.

"And," Marie continues, taking a bite of corn as she thinks. "No Low indicated." She nods like she's agreeing with herself.

Dad laughs. "My turn. High: Your mother is in a great mood today." They look at each other in that gooey, gross way, and

I pretend to gag. Dad throws his napkin at me. "Low: I got a nasty cut on my finger at work." He holds up his hand to show a big Band-Aid wrapped around the side of it. He's a carpenter, so he comes home with injuries a lot.

"Gross!" Marie says in awe. "Can I see it?"

"After dinner, maybe." Dad picks his fork back up. "How about you, kiddo?" They all look at me.

I clear my throat and move some food around on my plate. "Umm... High: I got a B on my social studies quiz."

"That's great. The one on the Industrial Revolution?" Mom asks.

I nod. "Umm... Low..." I falter a little, but I don't think anyone notices. "My presentation..." Again, I shovel mashed potatoes into my mouth so I don't have to talk anymore. This time I'm careful not to choke myself.

Mom looks at Dad and then back at me. "What happened, honey? I thought it went well?"

"I said it went fine. And it did. It's not a big deal."

I glance up from my plate, and Marie is scratching her nose. She clears her throat, trying to get Mom's attention. I kick her under the table, but she keeps doing it, raising her eyebrows and bobbing her head. Mom looks at her.

"Huh?" She touches her nose. "Is there something on my nose?"

"No!" Marie looks at me, then back at Mom, then at me again, in a way she must think is sly. All the while, she is still scratching her nose.

Mom turns to me, and I see the lightbulb go on. "Oh, honey." Her eyes soften. "Does this have something to do with the pimple on your nose?"

"Oh my God, Mom! I told you this morning. Can you please not say that word? It's so gross!" I throw down my silverware. "Like my face..." I mumble.

She and Dad exchange another look. "Oh, Emma." She reaches out to rub my arm. I shrug her off.

"It's fine. I'm fine." I pick my fork back up and take another bite. Mom and Dad look at each other *again*. "Can you stop looking at each other like that? I'm *fine!*" I practically shout.

"Emma, fine doesn't usually mean fine."

"Fine, ugh, I mean, okay. I'm..." I try to find a word besides fine. "Okay. I'm okay! Okay?" I see Marie and Dad exchange a covert glance out of the corner of my eye. "Can we please drop it?"

"Only if you promise to talk to me about it when you're ready," Mom says, still looking at me in that mom-like way.

"Yes, fi—I mean, okay." My eyes start to sting again, but I don't really know why. "Can I be excused?" I don't wait for an answer.

5:57 P.M.
BEDROOM

I've been staring at myself in the mirror, and I've decided I'm not *that* ugly, despite the zit on my nose.

My hair isn't horrible. It's brown, which is kind of boring, but it's not like a dull, mousy brown. It's more of a chestnut brown, I guess. It's a little wavy and falls above my shoulders.

My nose is a little pointy, but I wouldn't say it's witchy.

I have nice eyes. Especially after I've been crying. Although a little red and watery, they're also brighter. And I have a little freckle under my right eye. I think he's cute.

And, good news: I think my boobs may be growing. There's almost a bump under my shirt.

6:05 P.M.
LYING IN BED

Mom peeks her head into my room without knocking.

"Mom," I groan.

"What? Is it so bad that I want to check on you?" She comes over and perches on the edge of my bed. "Do you want to talk about it?" She reaches out to touch my leg, and I don't know why, but it makes me want to cry some more. The floodgates open.

"Oh, sweetie, come here." I lean into her arms, finding an odd sense of relief in her soft top half. She strokes my hair as I continue to cry.

When I finally get it all out, I lift my face from her chest.

"Sorry," I tell her as I swipe at my nose. "You're all wet."

"Don't be sorry, Em. Never be sorry for expressing your feelings." I put my head down on her shoulder. She rubs my back gently. "So…"

I sigh. "Audrey…" Mom doesn't say anything; she just keeps rubbing my back. "I had my argument presentation today." I feel Mom nod. "And I woke up with this big zit on my nose. I tried to cover it up, but I guess I didn't do a very good job."

Mom opens her mouth to say something. She must change her mind, though, because she doesn't actually say anything.

"During my presentation, everyone was scratching their nose." I sit up. "Like this." I show her the deliberate, top-of-the-nose scratch that Audrey did.

"Everyone?" Mom asks skeptically.

"No, I guess not *everyone*. Audrey, Zoe, Hunter…" My voice wavers.

Mom's forehead creases, and she closes her eyes. "Oh, Emma. I'm so sorry." She sighs. "Kids are horrible."

"Yeah…" I agree. "Why did you have any?"

"Because I got you. Not so horrible." She smiles as she moves a piece of my hair behind my ear. "I hope you know how wonderful you are, Emma." I force a bit of a smile. "Everyone gets zits."

"Thank you for not saying the p-word."

She laughs a little. "You're welcome. I mean it, though. You are beautiful, smart, kind, and compassionate. I hate to see you upset."

"Okay, okay, no need to get sappy, Mom."

"You know I can't help it."

I roll my eyes. "I'm fine, really." She raises her eyebrows at me. "I'm..." I think for a second. "I'm superb."

Mom laughs and stands up. "Okay, then." She walks to the door. "I love you, sweetie. I'll help you with your makeup tomorrow morning."

"Thanks, Mom."

When she closes the door, I flop back down on my pillows, staring at the ceiling but not really thinking about anything.

8:22 P.M.

I must have fallen asleep because it's dark out now. I'm also really hungry.

I open my door and walk quietly down the stairs. Mom, Dad, and Marie are watching TV in the living room. I go into the kitchen to get a snack.

I pop a piece of bread in the toaster and grab the peanut butter. While I'm waiting, I check my phone. I have a notification: *Cherrrrr_1001 tagged you in a photo.* I open it. It's Ruby and me jumping in the bathroom.

Bathroom Bonding! #BestFriends #ForgetThem #Forgetbullies #SupportSystem #Loveyouuuu @3mm_uh_16 @OG_RubyGirrl.

I leave a comment.

Awww, you guys are the best! #Biffles

My toast pops up, and I close the app.

8:25 P.M.
KITCHEN

I put my plate down and grab a glass of water. When I turn around, a bite is missing out of my toast.

"Seriously, Dad!" I shout.

"What?" he asks innocently from the other side of the wall.

"I can hear you crunching. That's rude."

He walks back into the kitchen. "I have no idea what you're talking about." He gives me his big, cheesy smile. I sit down to eat my toast.

"Everything okay, kiddo?" He sits down across from me.

"Yes, Dad. I'm sure Mom already told you everything. All is good." I give him a thumbs-up as I chew.

"Okay. Well, let me know if you want me to beat anyone up for you." He stands up and kisses the top of my head.

"I will. Thanks, Dad."

My parents can be alright sometimes. Keyword being *sometimes*.

9:17 P.M.
BACK IN BED

I feel like I've spent a lot of time in my bed today. I'm not even tired because I took that nap after my cry fest with Mom.

Ugh.

9:20 P.M.

I wonder if Mom was picked on. I know she didn't get boobs until high school. Dear God, please don't let that happen to me.

9:21 P.M.

I really do think they're starting to grow. Maybe I'll measure them tomorrow. How do you do that?

9:23 P.M.

Ruby has giant boobs. They were all over the place when we were jumping in the bathroom.

9:24 P.M.

I hope my boobs are giant.

9:27 P.M.

Why do boys have nipples?

CHAPTER 6

I want her eyes.

FRIDAY, APRIL 23RD
7:17 A.M.
BATHROOM

"Hold still," Mom scolds me. I'm sitting on the toilet seat (don't worry, the lid is down) while Mom puts makeup on my zit. Which is still large and in charge, day two.

Ugh.

"I feel like you're attacking me," I tell her.

"Do you want me to help you or not? I have to get ready too, you know."

"Okay, okay."

"Don't roll your eyes."

I don't bother saying anything to that.

"Alright, take a look," Mom says as Marie tries to squeeze herself into the bathroom with us.

I stand up and check my face in the mirror. I can still kind of see the zit. Its red face is hiding just beneath its warm blanket of makeup until he's ready to pop out and scare anyone who dares to face him—

"Hellloooo? Anyone in there?" Marie taps my head a couple times.

"Stop!" I swat her hand away.

"Well, let me in. I need to brush my teeth."

"Okay, girls, that's enough," Mom says half-heartedly. "What do you think, Emma?"

"Yeah, good. It's great. Thanks, Mom." I don't want her to feel bad for not being able to fully hide it. It's not her fault it's the biggest zit that's ever invaded someone's face.

Mom shuffles us out of her way so she can finish getting ready. I walk back to my room to do the same, leaving Marie, who's doing a little dance and humming while she brushes her teeth.

7:21 A.M.
BEDROOM

I stare at myself in my mirror. More specifically, at my zit. Why can't I have perfect skin like all the girls in the magazines and on TV? I know it's all photoshopped, and no one is that perfect in real life, but it doesn't make me want it less. I grab my phone. I see a text from Ruby in our group chat.

Ruby: Hey, Em. How's the face today?

Me: Well… it's still there, but my mom helped me put some makeup on to try and cover it up.

Cher: How'd that go?

I take a picture of myself to send them. I immediately hit "retake." I smiled, and it looked like I was trying too hard. I take a new one, sticking my tongue out.

Ruby: Definitely better!

Cher sends a thumbs-up emoji.

Me: I'll see you soon, Rubs. I'm gonna walk today.

Back in the mirror, my eyes are immediately drawn to my nose.

I open my phone again, so I can admire some beautiful people (even if I know it's unrealistic to want to look like them). I search #pretty and start scrolling.

I see a girl with flawless brown skin and dark brown eyes staring into my soul. A girl is swimming in a perfectly blue pool. I can't see her face, but she's slim and tan. Another girl is showing off her manicure, delicate gold rings shining on each of her fingers. Yet another girl is wearing tiny jean shorts and a bikini top. She has perfect cat-eye make-up and gorgeous beach waves in her hair, which is falling over her shoulder. I open her account. Her bio says, *It is what it is. Be yourself.* But the weird thing is, the pictures are not the same girl.

I scroll through a few of them and click on a close-up of a girl's eye. It has a blue outer rim, like the color of the ocean. Inside, it's like sea glass, fading from dark blue to greenish. The comment underneath says, *I want her eyes.* They *are* cool-looking.

I lean in close to my mirror to investigate my eyes. Mom says they're blue, but they're not. They're green.

Whoa. My eyes are like that girl's.

I examine the picture again. Yep, my eyes have a blue outline and kind of fade to green. How have I never noticed this before?

I take a step back and study myself. I must find ways to wear makeup that makes my eyes pop. I save the picture, so I can come back to it later. I check the time and realize I need to leave, like now, to meet Ruby. I grab my backpack and run out the door.

7:35 A.M.
WALKING TO SCHOOL

"So then, she starts yelling at *me* about my homework not being done, and I was like, 'Mom, you've officially lost it. I bet Dad would never—' And then she cut me off and told me to go to my room and not talk to her for an hour." Ruby's braids are pulled half-up today, and she flips them over her shoulder as she finishes her story.

Ruby's dad was in the army and died when she was five years old, so her mom is a single mother. I think she's super cool, but Ruby thinks she's crazy. She lets us call her by her first name, Georgia—how cool is that? She's young and pretty, she's the boss at her job, and she wears super sexy shoes when she goes out. She is pretty much the coolest adult ever.

I nod, eyeing Ruby.

"Why are you staring at me like that?" She takes a step away from me.

"Like what?" I ask innocently.

"Your eyes are super wide, and you keep blinking. Like an unnatural amount of blinking. Are you losing it, too? What is happening to the people I love?" She throws her hands in the air and starts mumbling gibberish.

"No! Stop. I'm fine." I pull her arms down, but she fights me. I pull harder and hold them to her sides. We stop walking.

"Maybe *you're* losing it," I tell her, still holding her arms down.

She thinks for a second. "That is a possibility," she admits. "But that doesn't explain why you're blinking so much."

I can't deny that. I was blinking a lot. I wanted her to notice my pretty eyes. I take my phone out to show Ruby the picture of the girl with sea-glass eyes.

"Ooh," she says, "her eyes are cool."

I blink. Ruby blinks back at me. She isn't noticing. I feel a flush of warmth on my cheeks.

"Do you think my eyes are kind of like hers?" I ask quickly.

She puts her face really close to mine. I can feel her breath on my face. "You know what… they totally are!" She puts her hand up for a high-five. "Cool!" She starts walking again. I pause for a second, then do a little gallop to catch up to her and her stupid, long legs.

Ruby bumps her shoulder against mine. "Want to sleep over tonight? We can try makeup like the girl in that picture."

I find myself smiling and bump her shoulder back. "Um, obv!"

8:04 A.M.
SCHOOL ENTRANCE

Ruby and I walk up to our usual morning spot, to the left of the school doors. Cher's not here yet.

"Was Cher at her dad's last night?" I ask Ruby. The only time Cher doesn't beat us to school is when she's with her dad. He lives like twenty minutes away, and she says they always get stuck in traffic. Her parents got divorced last year; that's why she transferred to St. Lucy's.

Ruby scrunches up her forehead to think. "Hmm, no, I don't think so. Wait." She thinks for another couple of seconds. After what seems like an unnecessary amount of thinking time, she says, "No, definitely not because when I talked to her last night about the math homework, I heard her mom talking in the background."

I nod and crane my neck to survey the area. Then I see a familiar blond head making its way toward us.

"There you are!" Ruby runs over to give Cher a hug. "We were getting worried." She lets Cher go from her embrace. Cher touches her hair to make sure it's still intact.

"It's fine," I assure her.

She nods and says, "I was over there talking to Audrey and Zoe."

My heart beats a little faster. "Why?"

"Don't be mad," she says, "but I was kind of telling them off about yesterday and the nose thing."

"Oh my God, Cher, come on! That's embarrassing." Ugh, they're probably laughing at me now, talking about how I need my friends to stick up for me. Apparently, I can only daydream about standing up to Audrey. As usual, my cheeks start to burn.

"It's not," she says matter-of-factly. "I didn't say anything about you or your feelings. All I said was that it was really uncool. Then I pointed out that last week, Zoe had a big pimple on her cheek, and no one made fun of her." She chuckles. "Then, I said I'd be sure to remember the next time either of them gets one. They rolled their eyes at me, but I could tell it made Zoe nervous. She always breaks out when her period is coming," Cher says with a smirk. "She kept looking at Audrey."

I ignore the fact that Cher used the p-word for *zit*. "Good," I say. "She's such a follower anyways. Do you think Audrey is nice to Zoe?"

"Probably not," Ruby says.

Audrey and Zoe are talking to each other, glancing over at the boys, who are, as usual, throwing a ball around. Why are boys so predictable?

"I think Zoe puts up with it," Ruby continues, "so she can be 'cool' with Audrey." She pauses for a second before turning back to us. "Why does popularity work like that?" She starts flailing her arms about. "Why are the 'popular' kids the ones who are mean to everyone? No one actually *likes* them. It makes zero sense." She looks back and forth between Cher and me, waiting for a response, her eyebrows sky-high.

It's actually kind of a good point. "Yeah," I agree, "but they're pretty, and they have nice stuff, and they have cool parties."

Ruby stomps her foot. "So are we, and so do we! What about my hotel birthday party last year?"

"It's called irony," Cher chimes in. "Remember? We learned about it last week in Ms. Stein's class." She looks at us expectantly. Ruby and I stare back, blank-faced. Cher sighs and shakes her head. "It's when something happens that is the *opposite* of what you expect. So, Audrey and Zoe are really mean to everyone else, but they're still seen as the *popular* girls."

"Ahhhh," Ruby and I say in unison. We look at each other and giggle.

Cher rolls her eyes at us as the bell rings. "Come on, weirdos."

12:16 P.M.
LUNCH

Cher and I are already sitting down when Ruby comes bouncing over with her lunch. She plops down onto her seat and says, "Cher, I almost forgot. Emma and I decided we should have a sleepover tonight. We're going to try to copy makeup styles. You in?" She wiggles her eyebrows up and down.

Cher thinks for a second. "Yeah, I should be able to. I'm at my mom's until Sunday."

"Excellent." Ruby takes a bite of her pizza. "Show her the picture, Emma."

When I show Cher the picture of the sea-glass eyes, she examines it for a couple of seconds. "I like it," she says.

"Don't her eyes look like Emma's?" Ruby prods. "Get real close." Cher doesn't get as close as Ruby did, but she does lean in and inspect my eyeballs.

"Yeah, they do," she says slowly. She sits back down, staring at me for another couple of seconds. She lifts her finger like she has an idea. "We need to make your eyes look bigger," Cher announces. "They're a little small—no offense. Honestly, I don't mean it's bad," she quickly adds.

"It's fine." I wave her comment away like it doesn't bother me. "It's true. I've always thought that. I didn't even realize my eyes were like that until I inspected them up close this morning." I shrug.

"Well, we're going to make them pop!" Ruby pokes her pizza slice at me.

Cher nods and then asks Ruby, "Do you think your mom will let us use the good stuff if we show her the picture?"

"Oh, definitely," Ruby says. "She loves making us feel like 'confident young women.' She's all about that female empowerment stuff."

I clap my hands at high-speed. "I'm so excited! Make me beautiful."

Ruby looks at me seriously. "You already are, Emma." She reaches out to touch Cher's hand. "And so are you, Cher." She smiles and puts her hand to her own heart, "And so are you, Ruby." We all lose it then. A few sixth-graders at the table behind us peer over, and Ruby sticks her tongue out and crosses her eyes at them, which makes us laugh even harder.

CHAPTER 7

I thought your presentation was cool.

"Emma, has anyone scratched their nose at you today?" Cher asks as we walk to math class.

"No, thank God."

"Good," she says.

"Good," Ruby says.

"Good," I say.

We burst into giggles again as I bump into someone and drop my books. Oh, geez. I drop down to the floor to pick everything up as quickly as I can. The person I bumped into does the same to help me. When I glance up, my heart starts pounding, and my cheeks light on fire. It's Connor. I immediately drop my head back down, hoping he won't see my red face.

"Here you go." He hands me my book and my pencil case.

"Thanks," I mumble. I stand up and start to walk over to where Cher and Ruby are waiting for me.

"Hey, by the way," he says, touching my arm. His arms are muscular, probably from throwing baseballs, and I can see little brown hairs covering them. "I thought your presentation was cool yesterday."

I didn't know it was even possible, but my cheeks burn hotter. Is he making fun of me? I'm too nervous to look up at him.

"Okay, well, see you later." He continues walking down the hall.

"Bye," I softly call after him. I scurry over to Cher and Ruby. "Oh. My. God!" I squeal.

"What were you guys talking about?" Ruby demands.

"Nothing really. He helped me pick up my stuff, and then he said my presentation yesterday was 'cool.' Do you think he was making fun of me?" I hope they don't hear the desperation in my voice.

Ruby answers immediately, "No, of course not. Your presentation *was* cool. Who doesn't love gifs of kittehs?" She says kitties in a fancy accent.

Cher takes a second. "I don't know... he is friends with Audrey." Ruby gives her the evil eye. "What?" she says. "I don't want to lie."

"That's true," I tell Cher. While I love Ruby for being supportive, Cher has a point. I need to be realistic. "Whatever. It doesn't matter. *Audrey* likes him, so you know they'll be going out soon enough."

"Ugh," Ruby moans. "Emma, you're a way cooler person than Audrey."

"Also true." I smile coyly. "How red was my face, though?" Cher and Ruby look at each other. I know it must've been bad then. "Uggghhhh. Why does my face do that?" I put my head down into my books but raise it back up immediately, so I don't embarrass myself by running into another person.

"Alright, everyone, listen up," Ms. Stein calls. "Who has their permission slips for the field trip to the health center?"

Oh, crap. I totally forgot about the permission slip yesterday with all my sulking about the zit. Speaking of, I wonder how it's holding up. Mom must have done a good job on the makeup because no one has scratched their nose at me all day.

Ms. Stein walks up and down the rows, collecting the signed permission slips. "If your parents have questions about the trip, please let them know they can call or email me."

"Ha!" Alejandra whispers from behind me, "I can imagine my mom calling. 'Hello? Is my daughter going to be learning about sex? Aren't they a little young for that?'"

I turn around to face her. "Well, that's better than mine, who would be like, 'Oh, this is great. Young people need to be educated. They need to know what's going on inside of their *bodies*.'" We giggle, and I turn back to my desk before Ms. Stein notices us.

Hunter calls out, "I'm really excited about this trip, Ms. Stein!"

"I'm sure you are, Hunter," she says sarcastically. Say what you want about teachers, but Ms. Stein isn't too bad. She doesn't get mad at people like Hunter, who make comments like that. She doesn't fall for it. Instead, she plays along.

"Permission slips are due by next Friday, my friends," she continues. "No exceptions. If you don't bring them, you'll be staying back with Mr. Jeffries, who will show you a video from the eighties covering the same topics."

Mr. Jeffries is our PE teacher. He has a lot of thick, dark arm hair, and he always, *always* has sweat stains in his armpits. I immediately take out my planner and write a note to remember my permission slip.

Ruby casually walks past my desk, pretending she needs a pen. She puts her hand out. "Do you think if Mr. Jeffries watches the video, it'll teach him about deodorant?"

I swat her hand away. "I hope so. Hey, do you think your mom will order us pizza tonight?"

"Ooooh yeahhhh," she says as she saunters back to her seat.

3:07 P.M.
WALKING HOME

"Mom." I call her on our way home.

"Emma."

"I have a question."

"I have an answer. Hopefully." She thinks she's funny.

I roll my eyes at Ruby. She sticks her tongue out at me. "Can I spend the night at Ruby's tonight?"

I hear the beginning of a sigh, so I cut her off before she can finish and plead, "Please? I need a girls' night after my traumatic experience yesterday!"

"That's true, but—"

I stop her again, "P-please! Cher's mom already told her it was okay." (She didn't. Cher had to go home and ask first, but I figured it would be helpful in my argument.) "And then if you say no, I'll be left out, which will create another traumatic event for me, and I'll be moping around the house all night—"

"Okay, okay." She doesn't let me finish this time. "You're right. A girls' night is always the perfect remedy. Are you coming home first?"

"Yes," I say calmly while also doing a little jig. "I need to grab my stuff."

"Okay, see you soon, sweetie. Love you."

"Love you too, Mom."

"Obviously, that was a yes?" Ruby asks.

I hold my hand up for a high five. She smacks it and then starts skipping. I laugh, watching her gain momentum before she does a cartwheel down the sidewalk. Her neon pink shorts flash against the dreary, springtime weather.

"Gross." She holds her hands up. They're covered in those little brown things that fall off trees. "These look like turds," she says, and then she throws one at me.

"Ew!" I dodge it. She pelts another one at me and starts running backward. I chase after her, stooping first to grab a couple of tree turds to retaliate with.

CHAPTER 8

Pizza forever!

Ruby's bedroom is so goofy. She has about a thousand stuffed animals on her bed. They're in a big heap in the corner. And she never makes her bed, so blankets are thrown every which way. She likes to keep it super dark, so her mom made her blackout curtains that keep out any sunlight. And, her walls are covered—and I mean covered—with posters. There's no real theme to the posters either. She has posters of bands, animals, nature, inspirational quotes, TV shows, and even one of a red car with a lady in a bikini standing next to it. She was especially proud of that one. It's right above her bed now.

The three of us—Ruby, Cher, and I—are sprawled out across Ruby's room. Cher's lying on the bed, I'm cross-legged in Ruby's "vintage" bean bag chair (really, it's just super old, but also super comfy), and Ruby is flat on her back on the floor.

"Okay, my turn," Ruby says. Her arms and legs are spread wide like she's making a snow angel. She pulls them tightly against her body. "Would you rather only eat pizza for the rest of your life *or* never eat it again?"

"Wait." Cher rolls onto her stomach to peer down at Ruby. Her blond hair spills over to cover her face. "Like, you have to eat pizza every day for the rest of your life?" She pushes her hair back behind her ear.

Ruby nods and springs back into the X-position. "Breakfast, lunch, and dinner. *Only* pizza. Or *no* pizza."

Cher rolls onto her back and stares up at the ceiling. "This is a hard one."

"No more pizza," I announce.

Ruby bolts upright. "Whoa, head rush." She puts her hand to her forehead for a second. "No more pizza?" she says as though I've offended her.

"What? I think I would get sick of it. Plus, then you'd never get to eat anything else. No more chocolate, no more ice cream, no more chips, no more pretzels—nothing!" I raise my eyebrows and shake my head. "I don't think I could do it."

"No one would miss pretzels, Emma," says Ruby, lying back down.

"Hey. I love pretzels," Cher says. She throws a stuffed owl at Ruby, who once again has her arms and legs zipped up against her body.

"That's why I said pretzels," I say, knowingly.

"Whatever," Ruby says, springing into an X again. "Pizza forever!" She lifts her arms and legs up in a salute to pizza.

"I think no more pizza, too," Cher says. "I get bored easily."

"Umm, hello!" Ruby sits up again, but slower this time, and places the thrown owl in her lap. She starts counting on her fingers. "Cheese, pepperoni, sausage, barbecue chicken, Hawaiian, that one with the gross-looking but delicious green stuff your mom makes, Cher."

"Pesto," she says helpfully.

"Yeah, pesto... ummm..."

"See!" I say. "That's only six. You'd be over it in a month."

"Ugh." Ruby sighs. "Maybe you're right. That's so sad."

Ruby's mom knocks on the door, and she waits for Ruby to say, "Come in," before she actually comes in. I wish my mom would do that.

"Pizza's here, girls," she announces.

"Mom. You have no idea how perfect your timing is." Ruby stands up and runs over to hug Georgia. "I almost never got to eat pizza again."

Georgia raises her perfect eyebrows at us. "What?"

"We were playing 'Would You Rather,'" Cher explains.

"Ah." Georgia puts her hands up. "Say no more. Come on. Pizza!"

7:06 P.M.
RUBY'S KITCHEN. EATING PIZZA.

"You know what, Ruby. You were right," I say after my fourth piece of pizza. "Pizza forever!" I raise my fist in the air.

"Pizza forever!" Ruby does the same, leaning into her chair and sliding backward a little. The only place I've seen kitchen chairs on wheels is at Ruby's house. When we were younger, Ruby and I would take turns pushing each other on them around her house.

"I don't know," Cher says. "I'd still miss pretzels."

"Oh my God, Cher," Ruby says. "You can crumble up some pretzels and put them on your pizza if you're going to miss them that much."

"Okay. Then I'm in." She raises her fist too.

"What are you dorks doing?" Georgia asks as she walks back into the kitchen. She opens the fridge, examining its contents for a second. With a sigh, she closes it and grabs a piece of pizza for herself. She changed out of her work clothes, and now she's wearing comfy harem pants and an army green tank top. She took her makeup off too, but she's as beautiful as ever. Her skin tone is a bit deeper than Ruby's and so smooth. Her round, dark brown eyes are outlined with long lashes that don't even need mascara.

"Saluting pizza," I tell her, reaching for one more slice.

She nods. "Makes sense."

"Mom," Ruby says, "can we use your makeup?"

"For what?" she asks suspiciously. She raises one eyebrow. First Ms. Stein and now Georgia, too? Is it an adult thing? I make a mental note to ask Mom if she can do it. I bet Dad can. He has the craziest eyebrows I've ever seen. Sometimes he lets me pluck the stray ones that poke him in the eye.

"Emma, show her the picture," Cher tells me. I pull it up and hand Georgia the phone.

"Well, this is classy," Georgia says. "Not too much, but enough to make her eyes pop."

"Emma's eyes are like the same color as that girl's, Mom," Ruby informs her.

Georgia comes over to check my eyes out. "And so they are. Let me see what I can spare for you ladies."

I turn back to my half-eaten pizza, but I'm suddenly too excited to eat it. If this goes well, maybe I can start doing my makeup like the girl, and then Connor will notice me and my beautiful sea-glass eyes, and we'll fall in love, and he'll kiss me...

"Earth to Emma!" Ruby waves her napkin at me.

"Sorry." I shake the dream off.

"What were you thinking about, Em?" Ruby asks. I can't stop a smirk twisting onto my face. "Ooooh now I know: Connorrrr," she playfully taunts.

I let the smirk turn into a full-on smile.

Across the table, Cher rolls her eyes. Why does she have to be like that? Ruby notices too.

"Cher. What's your problem?" she demands. Ruby stares straight at Cher, waiting for her response.

I hate confrontation. I hate fighting. Sometimes Mom will yell at me, and I'll just stand there quietly. Then I go up to my room and think about all the things I could have said.

Even here, I thought the same thing as Ruby, but I never would have said anything because I didn't want to start a fight. Ruby's not scared, though.

Cher purses her lips and doesn't say anything. Ruby continues staring at her.

"What?" Cher finally concedes.

"Why did you roll your eyes?" Ruby asks.

Cher sighs. "Don't get mad." My stomach turns over. That's never good. "I just think you're wasting your time pining over Connor," she finally spits out. Her green eyes meet mine. My cheeks light on fire. I can't help how I feel.

Now Ruby rolls her eyes. "Why? He wasn't part of the nose-scratching thing." She turns to me and nods encouragingly.

The reminder doesn't affect Cher. "That doesn't mean he *likes* Emma," she says, deadpan.

"But it doesn't mean that he *doesn't* either." Ruby stands up now, her hands on her hips.

I sit silently, my head swiveling back and forth between them. I don't want to be part of this conversation, even though it's about me. I don't know what to do, but I want it to end.

"Okay. Whatever," Cher says quietly, pushing her plate away from her. "This wasn't even what we were talking about."

Ruby sits back down, crossing her arms over her chest. Her boobs are so big she sort of rests them on her arms. I can still feel some tension in the room, but that happens with Ruby and Cher occasionally. They're both so opinionated and strong-minded. They'll get over it in a few minutes.

"How did you find that picture, Emma? Of the girl's makeup?" Cher asks.

I don't want to tell them that I was feeling ugly and wanted to admire pretty people. Instead, I tell them I found it on the Explore page.

"Hmm, okay," Cher says. "I was thinking we could each find an inspiration pic to try out tonight. Kind of like how yours has the same eye color as you."

"Ooooh, that's a good idea," I say. "There are a million makeup accounts. I'm sure we'll find something."

"Yeah," Ruby chimes in. "Let's go back to my room, though. I'm too full to look at this pizza anymore."

"But I thought pizza forever?" Cher half-heartedly raises her fist in the air, smirking at Ruby.

Ruby rolls her eyes but smiles. The tension lifts. "Yes, duh. But not every second of forever. Come on! Let's prettify!" She runs down the hallway.

7:36 P.M.
RUBY'S BEDROOM

"Ruby, stop moving!"

"I can't help it. You're poking me in the eyeball!" Ruby swats Cher's arm away. "You're too violent."

Cher snaps the eyeshadow case closed. "Okay, Emma, you do her eyeshadow. I might punch her." She flops down on the bed in a huff.

I step in front of Ruby, who is looking at me expectantly. "Close your eyes," I tell her. I open the case and pick up the little brush. I hover it over the different shades of brown, contemplating. I dab it in the lightest one and then lift it to Ruby's eye. I put the brush on her eyelid and sort of swirl it around, trying to be gentle. "I don't really know what I'm doing."

"That's okay," Ruby says. "At least you're not stabbing me." I put the brush down and give Ruby the hand mirror. Very quickly, she puts it back down and simply says, "We need help. Call in the reinforcements."

"Reinforcements?" I ask.

"Mom," "Georgia," Ruby and Cher say at the same time.

7:50 P.M.

Georgia expertly draws a black line across Ruby's eyelid, swooping it up at the end.

"How do you do that so perfectly?" Cher asks admiringly.

"A steady hand and years of practice." She hands the delicate, shiny black bottle to Cher. "Who's next?"

"Emma is," Cher says, already pulling supplies out of Georgia's makeup bag.

Ruby winks and blows a kiss at the mirror before hopping up out of the chair. I take her spot and wait for Georgia, who's discussing the benefits of full versus medium coverage foundation with Cher. I have little butterflies in my stomach. Why am I nervous?

8:02 P.M.

Georgia is a makeup magician. I look so cool.

To get the sea-glass eye look, she put white eyeliner on what she called my "water-line" to make my eyes look bigger. Then she put on eyeshadow primer (who knew that was a thing?), a base shadow, and then a subtle crease shadow. And she explained each step, so I could try to copy it myself next time.

"The key is for it to look natural. We're just highlighting your already beautiful eyes," Georgia said as she applied mascara. "Don't do more than two coats of this. It gets clumpy."

She paused, putting the finishing touches on with her mouth slightly agape. "Okay, check it out, Em."

My mouth falls open a little when I hold the mirror up. I can't help it. I'm pretty. And my eyes are so much bigger.

I take probably twenty-five pictures of myself while Georgia does Cher's makeup (she wants a Hollywood Glam look). I also try to copy the sea-glass eye girl's picture exactly. I think I get pretty close.

"Oh my gosh, yes, Emma!" Ruby exclaims when I show her. "That is so cool!"

I smile, content for once with my appearance. I'm going to ask Mom to take me to the store tomorrow and buy the makeup Georgia used, so I can practice with it. I don't think I'll ever be as good as her. I wonder if she would do my makeup like that every day. No. That's probably not reasonable.

I wish I could post these pictures, so everyone (Connor) could see my sea-glass eye makeup. But I also don't want people to think I'm too full of myself.

Someday, when I'm grown up and have boobs, I'm also going to be a makeup magician. And everyone (Audrey) is going to wonder why they were so mean to me back in the day. No one will ever remember my stupid nose zit.

8:22 P.M.

Ruby, Cher, and I stand together, admiring ourselves in the full-length mirror. Ruby's in the middle, with her arms around each of us.

"We look amazing," Ruby says.

"I believe my work here is done," Georgia says from the doorway. She takes a small bow as we shout our thanks.

The three of us turn back to our reflections quietly. Suddenly, Ruby shouts, "Let's wipe it off and try some more!"

12:26 A.M.

As fun as it was looking like the sea-glass eye girl, we had *a lot* more fun watching and trying different makeup tutorials. There was neon pink eyeshadow, teal lipstick, and contouring.

We posted a few pictures pouting our lips, each of us wearing a different shade of red lipstick. Cher "filled in" (Ruby and I prefer the more accurate term, "colored in") our eyebrows, and we all tried to do that eyebrow lift thing that Ms. Stein does. Cher was really good at it. Then we gave Ruby a unibrow, which she thoroughly enjoyed. She kept wiggling her eyebrows up and down at us.

"Stop it!" I laughed. "You look like you're trying to flirt with me!"

I ran away as she chased me around the house, shouting in a deep voice, "Help me pluck my eyebrow!" and, "Don't you like my eyebrow?"

Once we'd exhausted all the makeup options, we scrubbed our faces and finally convinced Ruby to get rid of her unibrow.

"I've gotten kind of attached to it," she said, petting it.

Now we're snuggled down. Ruby and I are sharing her bed, and Cher is on the air mattress.

"Maybe I should be a makeup artist when I grow up," Ruby says, yawning.

"I thought you wanted to be a music teacher?" Cher replies.

"Well, that's true." She sits up and leans over me. "I could do both. I could be a teacher during the week and then do people's makeup on the weekends, like for weddings and stuff."

"That would be a cool job," I say.

Ruby lies back down next to me and picks up a little stuffed turtle. She boops him on the nose. "Yeah, it would be," she says dreamily. She puts him with the others, smooshed against the wall in an attempt to make room for both of us in the bed. (It's a tight squeeze.) "I'm tired." She yawns again and rolls away from me. She sticks her butt out and wiggles herself to get comfortable.

"Ruby, don't be a bed hog!" I try to push her closer to the wall and get her butt away from me. She mumbles something incoherent back.

12:37 A.M.

"Emma," Cher whispers. "Emma. Are you awake?"

"Yeah." I roll over.

"Are you tired?"

"Sort of."

"I'm not." Cher's quiet for another few seconds, and then she says, "What's it like, having parents who are in love?"

"I don't know." I scooch up a bit to put my chin in my hand. Why is she asking me this? An image of my parents kissing in the kitchen floats into my brain. "Gross, I guess. They kiss all the time."

Cher doesn't say anything at first. "That sounds nice," she says even more quietly than before. "All I can remember about my parents being together is them fighting."

I hesitate. I don't want to say the wrong thing. Cher can be sensitive about the divorce still.

Her parents got divorced because her dad met someone else. In the year since then, her dad moved, married his girlfriend, and had a baby. It was a rough year for Cher. And her mom. Whenever Cher's at her dad's, she's usually babysitting or doing some sort of activity with his "new family," as she refers to them. Her mom recently started dating again, too. The last time she had a date, Cher called the guy a dingus.

Finally, I say, "That must have sucked."

"Yeah," she replies, "but sometimes I even miss that... because them being divorced sucks too." She pauses again. "Everything is different."

"Yeah," I say lamely, but I don't know what else to say. Cher rolls over on the air mattress, facing away from me now. I guess we're done talking.

1:04 A.M.

Ruby's snoring. But I'm still wide awake.

I always have a hard time falling asleep. There's so much running through my mind when I lie down. I think about what happened that day, what I wish had happened, possible future scenarios, boys (Connor), weird noises out on the street, robbers, natural disasters that occur in the night, Albus giving himself a bath at the foot of my bed, kicking Albus out—then all of a sudden, it's morning.

Cher is definitely in Snoozeville. Her breathing is slow and steady, and her blond hair is fanned out around her. She looks really pretty—like Sleeping Beauty. I realize after a minute or two that it would be super creepy if she woke up and I was staring at her, so I roll over to face Ruby.

I wonder why Cher asked me about my parents tonight. She doesn't talk about the divorce much anymore; last year she talked about it a lot. At our first sleepover with the three of us, she cried for a long time and then apologized afterward.

"Never apologize for your feelings, Cher," Ruby told her gently.

1:10 A.M.

Audrey pops into my head. I wonder what she did tonight. Did she hang out with Connor? I get a queasy feeling in my stomach when I imagine that. I can see them in my brain, watching a movie in Connor's basement, holding hands under a blanket so no one else sees them. The idea of it makes me want to scream. I feel a sudden urge to kick Ruby.

Instead, I change the scenario and imagine myself on the couch with Connor, holding hands under a blanket. I wonder if his hands are soft, or if they're beat up from playing baseball. I'm sure I'd like holding them either way. Then maybe he'd lean over and lightly touch my face. I'd look at him, and then he'd lean forward...

CHAPTER 9
Cool lipstick, Emma.

SATURDAY, APRIL 24TH
8:22 A.M.

"Good morning, sunshine!" Ruby yells as she hits me in the face with a pillow.

"Come on," I groan, rolling away from her and putting my own pillow over my head.

"You come on. I'm awake now!" She tries to pull my pillow away.

"Ruby, no..." Cher mumbles from below.

"Yes! It's moooorning!" she belts out in an opera voice, flinging her arms wide. "Let's go!" She pushes on my shoulder. She keeps pushing until I give in.

"Okay, okay, I'm up. I'm up," I say under my breath. I sit up and rub my eyes. Ruby leaps over me and plops down on the air mattress with Cher, who is not a morning person.

"I swear to God, Ruby, I will punch you if you touch me." They both stay perfectly still. Cher slowly turns her face up to Ruby's. Ruby smirks and boops her on the nose. Then she hops up and goes flying out of the room. Cher is on her tail within seconds.

I hear Ruby shout, "I give! I give!" Cher may be tiny, but she is surprisingly fast and strong. I take this opportunity to lie down again.

Cher comes strolling back into the room. She throws herself down next to me. "You have to sleep on the air mattress next time. I hate it. It makes so much noise every time I move." She pauses for a moment. "And it sounds like I'm farting all night."

"That's true. It does kind of sound like a fart." I accept that I'm not going to get any more sleep and sit up.

"Where's Ruby?" I ask.

"She's going to make pancakes," Cher says.

"Oh, no. We have to stop her," I say, scrambling out of bed.

"You know that's not going to happen." Cher starts rummaging through her bag.

For some reason, Ruby is obsessed with making us pancakes when we spend the night. Which is really nice. And I love pancakes. But Ruby's pancakes are either burnt to a crisp or still wet and gooey inside. There is no in-between. And she never lets us help. And she insists that we eat them.

"I have to try!" I shout heroically as I dash down the hallway.

8:40 A.M.

KITCHEN

I failed. Ruby's pancakes look like cooked sausage patties. We're sitting around the table eating cereal now. Ruby forced two pancakes down each of our throats before we convinced her they might kill us.

"All's you need is more practice, Rubs," Georgia says. She's drinking a cup of coffee and reading *Cosmopolitan*. The cover has a woman in a bikini on it (I think she's in some TV show about lawyers or the president or something). She's winking at the camera in a fun, flirty way. The headline reads *78 Insane Ways to Drive Him Wild!* Seventy-eight? Wow.

"I don't think they would have *killed* you guys," Ruby says grumpily. She picks up a Cheerio and throws it at me. I swat it away and shovel a big spoonful into my mouth.

"Who's to know?" Georgia says quietly, flipping the page in her magazine.

"Mom, can you not read your gross sex magazine around us?" Ruby snaps.

"Someone's a bit of a crabby patty this morning." Georgia flips another page in the magazine. "Plus, I don't know why you call it gross when you steal it as soon as I'm done."

Ruby narrows her eyes. "Whatever. It's gross that *you* read it. You're a mom."

"But I'm also a woman," she says, smiling up at us. "Women have needs." She winks.

"Ugh, even more gross." Ruby shivers.

Ruby is so lucky to have a mom as cool as Georgia. The only time my mom has talked to me about sex was when she explained how babies were made. That was a mortifying twenty minutes. Hearing your mom say "penis" is not something you can easily shake.

"I think it's wonderful that you're exploring your sexuality, Georgia," Cher says casually. Ruby almost spits out her cereal. I jerk my head up so fast I think I pull a muscle.

"Cher!" Ruby says, aghast. "Don't use the word 'sexuality' in front of my mother. Have you listened to nothing I've said? It's gross. She's gross!" She points across the table for reference.

Cher shrugs and goes back to her Cheerios.

"Ruby, it's not gross," Georgia says, putting the magazine down again and closing it.

Ruby puts her hand up. "Mom. Please don't start a spiel about the importance of knowing your body." She puts her hand down. "I already know." Her eyes are wide as she mouths, "I know." She shakes her head slightly before shooting back the last of her orange juice.

"I am a strong, confident, beautiful Black woman. It's nothing to be ashamed of." Georgia gives Ruby a pointed, motherly look and then stands up and puts her coffee mug in the sink. "Okay, ladies, I hate to be the bearer of bad news, but I've got to take you home in ten minutes. Ruby and I are going to get pedicures this morning." She walks down the hall to her bedroom

See? So cool! My mom never takes me to get a pedicure.

9:19 A.M.
RUBY'S LIVING ROOM

There is one thing Georgia and my mom have in common—always running late. It's been twenty minutes since we had ten minutes to get ready to go.

"Mom!" Ruby bellows down the hallway. "Come. On!"

"I'm coming. I'm coming," she says, walking out into the living room. She is so beautiful. I think Ruby is going to look exactly like her when she grows up. If you see pictures of Georgia as a teenager, you'd think it was Ruby.

Now, Georgia's braids are coiled into a big bun on top of her head. She's wearing some mascara, but besides that, no other makeup. Not like she needs it anyways. She's wearing black leggings and a long tank top that has an elephant walking out of a burst of rainbow colors. She smoothly slides on her jean jacket as she grabs her keys from the table by the door. "Let's rock and roll, ladies." I make a mental note to search *elephant t-shirts* later.

3:41 P.M.
LIVING ROOM

My phone buzzes. Albus and I were snuggling on the couch, but the noise scared him. He leaps off, stabbing me with his claws. "Ouch!" I shout as he sprints away. I pick up my phone. It's a text from Ruby in our group chat.

> Ruby: Emma. Check your picture from last night.

I don't respond and do exactly as she says. I have a new comment notification. It's the picture of Cher, Ruby, and me making kissy faces with the red lipsticks on. My heart drops into my stomach when I see who it's from: Capt_Connor. Fingers trembling, I tap to read the comment.

Cool lipstick, Emma, it says, with an "a-okay" emoji. I'm alone, but my cheeks flush. I put the phone in my lap and my hands on my head. My heart is racing, but I'm smiling. Connor! Connor commented on my picture! And he didn't say, *Cool lipstick, Ruby, Cher, and Emma.* He said, *Cool lipstick, EMMA.* I open it again to make sure this is real.

It's still there.

> Me: OH. MY. GOD. Ohmygodohmygodohymgod!!

Ruby texts back almost immediately.

> Ruby: I KNOW!! I told you he could like you, Em!

> Me: I don't know. He probably just likes the lipstick.

Ruby: Don't be stupid. Boys like Connor don't like lipstick. This is a sign! I even asked my mom, and she agrees.

Me: What should I say back?

My fingers are shaking, poised over the keyboard. I can't believe this is happening. I look around the room. No one's here. I want to tell someone about this. I want to tell everyone!

"Albus!" I hop up off the couch to try and find him. He's in the kitchen, licking something in the sink. "Stop that, naughty boy." I pick him up and snuggle him close. "Guess what? A boy might like me!" I hold him out in front of me. His round green eyes stare back. He's got crumbs in his kitty beard. I give him a kiss on his cute little nose. He wriggles out of my grip and once again sprints away, this time up the stairs.

I go back to the couch and flop down. I check my phone for a message from Ruby to tell me what to say. I am not good at playing it cool. No response yet.

I start making a mental list of what I could say back to Connor's comment:

- *You're 2 sa-weet!* with the winky-kissy face emoji? No way, too obviously flirty.

- *Thanks, it was Ruby's mom's lipstick.* No. Too aloof. He'll think I don't care.

- *You should taste it!* Oh my God, who do I think I am? Mom would kill me if I ever said something like that.

- *Aw, thanks @Capt_Connor!* with the monkey emoji covering his eyes? That might work.

I send the last idea to Ruby and Cher and wait for one of them to respond.

3:50 P.M.
Why haven't either of them said anything? I may have to do this without them. I don't want Connor to think I'm ignoring his comment. What if he thinks I don't like him because I took too long to respond? *I can't let that happen!*

But I also don't want to look like an idiot because then he might decide I'm a loser, and he shouldn't like me.

I will give them three more minutes.

3:53 P.M.
What are they doing?

3:54 P.M.

```
Ruby (Finally!): I think that's perfect, Em!

Me: What took you so long to respond?

Ruby: Emma. It's literally been four minutes…
```

I check the time I sent the message. She's right.

```
Me: It felt a lot longer in my brain!
```

I open the picture and type *Aw, thanks @Capt_Connor!* with the monkey emoji covering his eyes. I pause before I submit it.

What if I sound stupid? What is he going to think? Will he be able to tell I agonized over these three words? Does he really like me? Or is he messing with me? I swallow the lump in my throat. Whatever. I'm doing it. I put my phone down on my lap and let out a squeal, kicking my legs against the couch. Yeeee!

4:20 P.M.

My phone buzzes again, and I scramble to check it.

> Cher: That's cool Emma. But honestly, I wouldn't read too much into it.

My heart, which has been whirring for the last half hour, feels like it freezes.

> Me: Why?

Heat creeps up my neck. Did I get excited over nothing? Did Ruby and I read this situation totally wrong? Should I have ignored the comment? Oh, God. Oh, God. Oh, God.

> Cher: I mean, yeah, I guess he might like you, but it could also be that he thinks the picture was funny.

> Ruby: Yeah, but he specifically said Emma's name. I think that means something.

I don't say anything. I'm too nervous. My heart is whirring again.

> Cher: That's true… Idk. I just don't want you to get your hopes up if nothing happens.

Why does she keep saying that? I close my eyes for a second. When I open them, I furiously type out a message.

    Me: Why? Because you think he should like
    you instead?

But I chicken out and delete it. Instead, I shove my phone under a pillow on the couch and turn on the TV. I don't want to think about this anymore.

9:01 P.M.
BED

I spent the rest of the day hanging out with my family. Mom suggested a family movie night, which sounds totally lame, but it was actually really fun. We popped some popcorn, and Dad went out to get everyone's favorite candy: Reese's for me, Milk Duds for Marie, Snickers for Mom, and M&Ms and Swedish Fish for himself. We made a big nest of blankets and pillows and watched the movie on the floor.

It was easy. I didn't have to worry about what I looked like, what I said, or what I did. And I didn't have to think about Connor. Except during the lovey-dovey parts in the movie. But that was less about the comment and more daydreaming about being in love.

Now that it's over, though, I don't have the distraction. I'm going to go to bed so I can get up early tomorrow and be productive. I'll do my homework, and Mom's going to take me to get some new makeup.

11:02 P.M.

I'm still awake.

Why would Connor leave that comment specifically saying my name if he didn't want me to think he liked me?

11:48 P.M.

Why isn't Cher being supportive? I guess I should appreciate that she's always honest, but sometimes, I just want her to go along with what we're thinking. It's kind of annoying.

Is it so hard for her to believe that Connor might like me?

11:52 P.M.

Maybe she's jealous. She's the "pretty one" with her beautiful blond hair, bright eyes, and of course, boobs. You'd think she'd be the one boys are paying attention to. So maybe she's jealous it's me. That Connor is paying attention to me.

12:07 A.M.

Ugh. That's so lame. Why can't Cher be happy for me? She can't always be the center of attention. I love her, but she needs to get over herself.

Whatever. I'm going to ignore it.

12:19 A.M.

But I'm definitely going to tell Ruby my theory. She'll know what to say.

CHAPTER 10

This is... interesting.

MONDAY, APRIL 26TH
7:33 A.M.
WALKING TO SCHOOL

"What do you think?" I ask Ruby. I started spewing my thoughts on Cher being jealous about the whole, Connor-might-like-me thing as soon as she walked out her front door.

"It's... interesting." She bites her lip, thinking hard. "But I don't know. Do you think Cher is really that self-centered?" Her brown eyes are soft. "I think she wants to be honest is all it might be. It's good that we have a friend who's always so realistic."

"Or pessimistic," I say under my breath. "Don't you think her reaction to Connor's comment was weird on Saturday?" Ruby picks up a big stick and waves it around like a wand. "And she's been kind of distant since then," I add. "We didn't hear from her at all yesterday!"

"She was at her dad's," Ruby reminds me.

It's funny because Cher and Ruby definitely butt heads sometimes (like at our sleepover) but Ruby is fiercely loyal. She's not going to hop on board with my theory unless she really believes it.

I sigh. Maybe she's right. Maybe I'm overthinking all of this. Ruby turns to me, pointing her stick-wand at my hand, "Accio high-five!" Then she puts her hand up. I slap it.

"You're a weirdo."

"I know. But you love me."

I hip-bump her in response.

8:05 A.M.
OUTSIDE THE SCHOOL DOORS

Ruby and I are minding our own business, arguing about who's a better singer, Stephen or James from Celsius, when I see a gaggle of boys approaching out of the corner of my eye. Instinctively, I turn my head to inspect the group, searching for Connor. He's at the front, talking to Hunter. He runs his hand through his wavy, dark, messy-in-a-cute-way hair, and my heart flutters. I shake it off. I'm about to tell Ruby that while Stephen sings lead more often, James's parts are more heartfelt, but then, something miraculous happens.

As the group of boys passes us, Connor turns back. He doesn't stop walking, but he looks directly at me. He says, "Hey," and then smiles. At *me!*

My heart drops, and my breath catches in my throat. My cheeks warm. But before I can compose myself enough to say, "Hey," back, he's already gone.

I turn to Ruby, and we stare at each other for a couple of seconds before bursting into giggles.

8:17 A.M.
HALLWAY

Cher comes sprinting down the hallway. "I hate coming from my dad's," she complains as she opens her locker.

"We've still got a couple of minutes," I tell her.

Cher doesn't respond. She shoves her jacket and backpack into her locker and grabs her books. I'm waiting for her to get situated before I tell her about Connor. I want her full attention. She turns around and smiles at me. "Hi. Sorry, crazy morning." She runs her hand through her hair. She must have curled it. How is she so good at that?

I forget about Connor for a minute.

"Your hair is amazing." I self-consciously touch my own. I'm not having a bad hair day, but it isn't great either. It's a little frizzy and pulled half up, like it is most days. I wanted to do one of those little top knot buns that are messy and cute at the same time, but I can't seem to get the cute part.

"Thanks," Cher says. "My dad bought me one of those wand curlers. It's seriously ah-mazing. I'll show it to you next time you're over. Your hair would look great like this."

"Okay, cool!" I say brightly. Ruby was right. I was totally overthinking this whole Connor jealousy thing.

12:15 P.M.
LUNCH

"So," Cher starts as she opens her lunch. "I've been thinking about this Connor thing." My heart starts racing. Ruby and I quickly glance at each other and back at Cher. "It seems to be out of nowhere. I wasn't trying to be mean yesterday. But when do you ever even talk to him?" She tilts her head to the side, waiting for my answer.

My heart does a flip-flop. Connor! I forgot to tell her. "Connor said hi to me this morning," I say matter-of-factly. "Outside. Before you got here."

"Oh. Really?" Cher leans back in her chair, frowning slightly. "Why didn't you tell me before?" She looks at me curiously, her green eyes slightly narrowed.

Warmth spreads in my chest. I shrug. "You were all frazzled about getting here late. I figured I'd tell you later." I break off a piece of my peanut butter sandwich, trying not to smile. "Ruby was there."

Ruby nods. "Yes. I was. There." She smiles at me and nods again.

Cher starts nodding, too. "This is... interesting," she says slowly. "We need to analyze it further." She takes a bite of her sandwich. "Maybe we can do some research too. Can you hang out after school?"

For someone so doubtful that Connor might like me, she's taking one "Hey" pretty seriously. Not that I mind, though. It's nice to feel the spotlight, and for once, it's not the cause of embarrassment.

Ruby gazes off into the distance for a second and then turns back to us with a smack on the table and a "Yes!"

I follow her lead and also smack the table. "Yes!"

Cher rolls her eyes but smiles too.

I let the ball of excitement in my chest grow a little bigger.

4:28 P.M.
BEDROOM

Ruby, Cher, and I are sitting in a circle on my bedroom floor, ready to do some "research" (as Cher is calling it).

First, we try to remember every interaction I've had with Connor, ever—from bumping into him in the hallway last week and being on the same hockey team in PE to saying hello to me this morning. Cher is writing things down in a notebook decorated with cats wearing glasses.

For what feels like the hundredth time, we go through every detail of my interaction with Connor this morning.

"And he didn't talk to you at all the rest of the day?" Cher asks, her eyebrows raised and pink pen poised.

I shake my head. Why didn't Connor say anything to me the rest of the day? Why would he say hi and then nothing else at all? If Ruby hadn't witnessed it, I might have convinced myself I imagined the whole thing.

"Okay, interesting." Cher writes something down in the notebook. Interesting seems to be her new favorite word. She's said it about five thousand times. "Anything to add, Ruby?"

Ruby's reading a book, seemingly bored with the conversation.

"Nope, that pretty much sums it up," she says, snapping the book closed. "We know what happened. Let's move on to something else." She leans over and lightly taps her shoulder against mine.

I smile gratefully and let out a sigh of relief. This morning was exciting, don't get me wrong, but there are only so many times I can explain a two-second interaction. Even if my whole world stopped when it happened.

Next, we go through all of Connor's pictures to see if we can find out anything new about him. There isn't much to find, though. Most of his pictures revolve around baseball or his friends. What we do discover is that Audrey comments on literally every photo Connor posts.

"That seems a little desperate to me," says Ruby.

Cher thinks for a second. "Maybe a little, but I mean, it's kind of smart too. I read in *Cosmo* once that you should never let a guy forget that you exist."

"That's stupid," I say.

Cher looks at me quizzically. "Do you have any experience getting boys to like you?"

That one stings. "Well... no," I stammer. My cheeks warm.

"I didn't think so." Cher returns to stalking Connor's photos. "Let's go to Audrey's profile next. I wonder if Connor ever comments on her pictures." Ruby and I glance at each other. Cher is acting insane. But I'm curious, so we move on.

Connor has left only one comment on any of Audrey's photos. It's a group picture from the last school dance—Audrey, Zoe, Connor, Hunter, and a few others were in it. He said, *Good times!*

We decide after the picture stalking that it's time for a snack break. Marie is in the kitchen, still working on some homework.

"What are you guys doing up there?" she asks.

"None of your business," I tell her, grabbing a bag of pretzels and some peanut butter.

"Whatever," she says. "It's probably boring anyways."

"We're actually doing some detective work," Ruby says conspiratorially, sliding into the chair next to Marie. Marie's eyes are wide, interested; they flick to me for a second. I turn away. I am not telling her anything.

She turns back to Ruby. "About what?"

"Unfortunately, I can't tell you. Friendship Honor Code." Ruby salutes.

"You guys are weird," Marie says, returning to her homework.

8:37 P.M.
After all of our work today, we don't really have any new information. Except that Cher should be an investigator. She took this all very seriously.

But she never actually said, "I think he likes you, Emma."

8:56 P.M.
Why couldn't Connor like me? I have good qualities. I don't smell bad. I'm smart (when I try). I'm nice to people. I like to laugh. I have sea-glass eyes. I can sing the ABCs backward.

9:03 P.M.

On the other hand, I have no boobs, I don't know how to do my makeup, my face gets red whenever I get even slightly embarrassed or speak to a boy, I couldn't hit a baseball to save my life, I get zits on my face, I'm not super confident...

9:30 P.M.

Whatever. I'm awesome. "Forget them!" remember?

9:33 P.M.

But just in case, I'm going to have Mom put mascara on me in the morning.

CHAPTER 11

You look nice today.

TUESDAY, APRIL 27TH
8:16 A.M.
LOCKERS

I'm trying to examine the back of my head in my locker mirror to make sure I don't have any hair sticking up when Connor walks by and says, "Hey, Emma. You look nice today."

I freeze, my arm hanging in the air near my head. I think I black out for a second. I stare at Connor, unable to speak, cheeks flaming. He keeps walking toward class. Oh my God. *Oh my God!*

Cher is also watching Connor walk away, her mouth slightly agape. She turns back to me. "Maybe he *does* like you."

I put my arm down, and turning back to my locker, I whisper, "Oh my God." I grab my books with shaky hands and hold them tightly to my (flat) chest. Cher is still staring at me. I squeal, "Yeeee! Let's go. We have to tell Ruby!"

8:19 A.M.
ENGLISH

"Ruby!" I half whisper-half yell as Cher and I walk into Ms. Stein's class. I'm so excited, I'm shaking a little. Audrey watches as I speed walk to Ruby's desk. "You are never going to believe what happened."

Cher walks up calmly behind me but doesn't say anything. "What? Oh my God, what?" Ruby looks from me to Cher excitedly. She stands up. "Did you win something? Are we going to meet someone famous? No. We're going to a water-park for your birthday!" She hops up and down on her toes.

"What? No." I shake my head. "In the hallway—" The bell rings and cuts me off. I try to finish my sentence, glancing around to make sure no one is eavesdropping. "Connor—" Ruby claps her hands with anticipation, but we're cut off once again, this time by Ms. Stein.

"Ladies, have a seat," she says to Cher and me.

"Can I tell Ruby something really quick?" I ask as Cher goes to her seat.

Ms. Stein looks skeptically over her shoulder. "Don't you two walk to school together? Why didn't you tell her then?" How does she know that? "I know everything," she says in response to my blank stare. "Go sit down."

"Ugh," I sigh quietly. I drag myself over to my seat as Ms. Stein projects a writing prompt. Still, I feel like I'm walking on clouds. My cheeks are pleasantly warm, and my heart is gently thumping against my (still flat) chest.

8:49 A.M.

Once we're working on the writing assignment, Alejandra leans forward and whispers, "I heard a rumor."

I whip my head around, narrowing my eyes at her. "What did you hear?"

She sits back in her seat, satisfied by my reaction. "Something about Connor…" she pauses for dramatic effect, "and you." She raises one eyebrow. (Why can everyone but me do that?) I don't say anything. I just stare at her. She stares back.

"Are you going to tell me?"

"Why should I?" She takes off her black, square-frame glasses. I notice her bronze skin is as smooth and clear as glass. I wish my skin looked like that.

"Fine." I turn back to my assignment, which I'm actually kind of getting into.

9:10 A.M.

Alejandra pokes me in the back with her pen. I ignore her. I'm not playing this game. She can either tell me or not. Ms. Stein walks past to check on our work.

"This is very good, Emma. Careful of run-on sentences, though. You use a lot of commas, but they can't always hold two complete thoughts together."

I nod, rereading what I've already written.

Ms. Stein moves on to Alejandra. "Excellent descriptions, Alejandra. I feel like I'm there with your character." She smiles. "You're a very talented writer."

"Thanks," Alejandra says quietly. Ms. Stein starts walking toward Hunter, who's waving his arm in the air obnoxiously.

Alejandra pokes me again and whispers, "Emma."

I turn around. "What?" I say through clenched teeth.

"Emma? Do you need something?" Ms. Stein is giving Alejandra and me her stern-teacher look. Neither of us responds. I put my head down and start writing again.

"I'll tell you after class," Alejandra whispers.

9:15 A.M.

The bell rings, and I slowly pack up my books, waiting for Alejandra. Ruby and Cher both wait at the door for me. I wave my hand to tell them I'll see them in class. Cher gives me a quizzical look, but I ignore it and turn back to Alejandra.

"Soooo?"

She looks up like she's surprised I'm there. "Oh, right. Sorry for messing with you before. It's kind of fun knowing gossip." She smiles with her mouth closed. I wait for what she has to tell me. "Let's walk. We don't want to be late." She's quiet as we leave Ms. Stein's room, heading toward science.

"Soooo?" I ask again. "Are you going to tell me anything? Or are you going to make me guess?" I'm starting to get annoyed.

"Right. Sorry." She quickly scans the hallway to make sure no one is listening. "I overheard the boys talking outside this morning. I wasn't really paying attention at first, but then I heard your name, and my ears sort of perked up—"

I interrupt her. "Why?"

"Huh?" Her brown eyes are confused. "Why what?"

"Why did you start listening when you heard my name?"

"Oh." Her gaze shifts to the floor, and she almost runs into Laney Lindt, who's bent over in the hallway, tying her shoe. I grab Alejandra and pull her out of the way. "Oy! Thanks. Um, anyway, I don't know. I guess it's 'cause I think you're cool, and I like making fun of things with you. Whatever... Do you want to know what I heard or not?"

Hmm. I guess Alejandra and I do make comments about things Hunter will blurt out, or like the field trip the other day. I like Alejandra. She's nice. "No worries," I tell her. "I was surprised, is all. I think you're cool, too."

"Cool," she says, smiling back at me. She raises her eyebrows and shakes her head slightly, "Soooo..."

"Yes, yes! Continue!" I'm ready to jump out of my skin. This better be good.

"I couldn't hear much, from my spot on the ground—"

"Why were you on the—"

"Stop interrupting me!" I keep my mouth shut in response. "So I decided to get up and move closer. They didn't even notice." She rolls her eyes. "I stood behind Hunter, and he was like, 'So what are you gonna do about it, man?' And Connor was all like, 'I don't know, get her number?' And then they all starting hoo-ing and ha-ing, being typical, stupid boys."

I stop dead in my tracks in the middle of the hallway. Laney almost runs into me. "Stop it," I say, dead-pan. Alejandra looks at me over her glasses. "Are you for real? Is he going to ask me for my number?"

Alejandra shrugs nonchalantly, but there's a slight upturn at the corner of her mouth.

"Oh my God." I'm ready to start squealing when I realize the hallway is starting to clear. "Oh my God!" I say again, but for a different reason this time. "Come on! We're going to be late!" I grab Alejandra by the arm, and we sprint down the stairs to Mrs. Short's room.

9:18 A.M.
SCIENCE

Alejandra and I make it into class about a half-second before the bell rings. We're both slightly panting as we flop into our respective seats. Me up front, next to Ruby. Alejandra toward the back, next to Cher, actually. I never realized that before.

"Get started on your bellringer, ladies and gentlemen," Mrs. Short calls from her desk in the back of the room. "You have five minutes."

I take out a pencil and open my notebook to get started when Ruby elbows me.

"Ow! What was that for?" I flick her on the arm in retaliation.

"What were you talking about with Alejandra? And what did you have to tell me before English? Why are you leaving me in the dark about everything?" Ruby whines, throwing her head back and pretending to cry. She lifts it up after a second and says, "Dish."

I put a finger up to signal "wait a second" and write in my notebook.

1. Connor told me I looked nice before class this morning!!

2. Alejandra told me that Connor is going to ask for my number!!

I nudge Ruby and casually point at my list of exciting news with the eraser of my pencil (which happens to be a little bear). She reads it quickly and then slowly looks up at me, beaming.

"Shut up!" she whisper-yells. She starts doing a little jig in her seat, and I join her.

"Girls!" Ruby and I both jerk our heads up at the sound of Mrs. Short's booming voice. "What did I say about putting the two of you next to each other?" She pauses, eyeing us over her glasses. "Get to work!" she says before turning back to Laney Lindt, who she's talking to at her desk.

I hear Audrey snigger from her seat two rows behind us. I peek over my shoulder, and she gives me a nasty look. But it doesn't even faze me. I sneak a smile at Ruby, who winks back, and I actually get started on my bellringer.

Connor wants my phone number!

CHAPTER 12

I hope Audrey is seeing this.

TUESDAY, APRIL 27TH
9:30 A.M.
SCIENCE

I feel like we've been in class for hours, but we've only been sitting here for twelve minutes according to the clock. Which means only one minute has passed since I last checked. Mrs. Short is droning on about some sort of project we're going to be doing.

I wonder when Connor is going to ask for my number. At lunch? After school? What do I say? Do I literally say the number? Do I put it in his phone for him? Do I write it down on a little scrap of paper, like they do in old movies? I rip a little corner off the assignment sheet in front of me (that I have read none of), and I write my phone number as neatly and cutely as possible. Just in case.

9:48 A.M.
STILL SCIENCE

What will we talk about? I don't know anything about baseball. I take out my planner and write in the notes section, *Learn about baseball.*

9:59 A.M.
STILL, STILL SCIENCE

The project Mrs. Short was explaining is to build a roller-coaster. We have the last ten minutes of class to pick a partner and brainstorm.

Cher comes over to our desks, and we're about to do Rock, Paper, Scissors to see who has to work alone. That's the hard part about a group of three best friends—when we have to work in partners, teachers never let us switch it up for a group of three, so one of us is left out. Before we can start, though, I hear Audrey's nasally voice.

"Connor!" She traipses over to his desk, putting her hands down and leaning toward him. "Do you want to be my partner?"

Connor glances at Hunter, who's standing next to his desk. Hunter covers his face with his hand and turns away from them.

"Um... I think I'm going to work with someone else, Audrey," he says, rubbing his neck.

Flabbergasted, Audrey stands there for a second. Hunter snorts, leaning on Connor for support.

Connor gives her a half-hearted, "Sorry," before she violently turns and grabs Zoe by the wrist. They make a beeline for a table in the back, Audrey whispering angrily.

I blink a couple times. I can't believe Connor said no. I almost feel bad for her. (Keyword being *almost.*) It's her own fault, really, for asking loudly enough for, like, the entire class to hear. Which I'm sure she did because she thought he was going to say yes.

Next to me, Ruby stifles a giggle. Cher and I exchange stunned looks.

"Everyone should have their partners figured out by now," Mrs. Short announces.

There's a tap on my shoulder. I turn around and freeze.

"Hey," Connor says, glancing at Ruby and Cher behind me.

"Hi." Suddenly, I'm very aware of my arms. What do I do with them? Why are they hanging like that? I cross them. That still feels weird, so I uncross them. Then I put one hand on my hip. *What is wrong with me?*

"So, uh, do you have a partner for this rollercoaster project?" I stare at Connor's beautiful, tanned face and his baby blue eyes. He runs his hand through his dark hair, ruffling it a little. Is he nervous? No way. My heart is pounding in my chest. There may be some sort of drum practice happening in there. I wonder if Connor can hear it.

"Uh, that's what we were trying to figure out." I point to Cher and Ruby behind me. My face is on fire, or at least it feels like it is. "There's three of us, which sucks..."

"Well, maybe you could work with me?" Connor says. I think my mouth falls open. "Then your friends can work together, and no one is by themselves."

Is this really happening? The little drum players in my chest are beating so hard, I think they're going to break out. I might die right here. I peek over my shoulder at Cher and Ruby, who are staring at us, wide-eyed.

"Yeah, um, sure, uh... that would be great. Cool. Yeah," I eventually manage to spit out.

"Okay, cool." Connor pulls his phone out of his pocket. "So, um, I'll probably need your number. In case we need to talk about the project." He hands his phone to me. "Want to put it in?"

"Totally." I hope Audrey is seeing this. I take the phone, and, hands shaking, I put in my number and my name. I hand the phone back to him and smile nervously down at my feet.

"Cool," Connor says again. He glances over at Ruby and Cher behind me and then over his shoulder at his friends, who are huddled by the door, watching us. "So... I'll text you later?"

"Yeah!" I say a little too loudly. *Take it down a notch, Emma.* I tone it down a little and add, "Definitely." He smiles, and my heart skips a beat. As he starts backing away, I throw in a small wave before turning back to Cher and Ruby. I saw someone do that in a movie once, and it was so cool—casual yet flirty.

Cher and Ruby are still staring at me. Ruby's mouth hangs slightly open but quickly turns into a wide grin. Cher slowly says, "Oh. My. God." The bell rings, and everyone around us starts shuffling out of the room. I cover my face, and the three of us jump up and down, shrieking.

"Everything okay, ladies?" Mrs. Short calls over, smirking.

"Yep. Great!" I tell her. We grab our books and fly out of the room.

LUNCH

"Okay, but did you guys happen to look over at Audrey while I was talking to Connor? Was she watching? Did she see it happen?" I am practically begging for them to say yes.

"I was too busy watching you!" Ruby shouts.

"Oh my God, Ruby, stop shouting," Cher says.

"Sorry," Ruby says, not sounding sorry at all. She's been beaming at me all morning. "I am. So. Excited." She claps her hands on each word for emphasis. "About all of this," she adds, waving her arms around.

"I know." I'm trying to be nonchalant, but I can't stop smiling. "I can't believe it. I wish I could have seen Audrey's face, though. Serves her right for being such a witch all the time." I crane my neck, trying to find her in the lunchroom.

Cher's picking at her sandwich. She puts it down and looks up at me. "I'm honestly shocked. I did not see that coming."

I stop searching for a distraught Audrey. "I know," I say with a laugh. "Me neither." I pop a Dorito in my mouth, thinking for a second. It feels good. For once, something exciting is happening to me.

"No, really. I can't believe it." Cher shakes her head. The emphasis on how shocked she is rubs me the wrong way, but I brush it off. Honestly, I'm as surprised as her.

"I mean, we don't know for sure that he likes me. He only asked to be my partner on this project, not for me to be his girlfriend." This realization hits me only as I say it out loud.

"He could be after your brains," Ruby agrees.

Ugh. I put my head down on the table.

"Oh, don't be stupid," Cher reprimands us. "He obviously likes you, or he would have let Audrey be his partner. Or Hunter. Or one of the other boys."

I think about this for a second. "True," I concede. "But it still doesn't mean he wants to be my boyfriend."

"Let's stay optimistic," Ruby says. "You should practice your makeup tonight and wear it to school tomorrow!"

"Ooh! Good idea!"

3:06 P.M.

I saw Connor in the hallway after lunch, and he smiled at me. I still can't wrap my mind around the fact that he might like me. Audrey also kept shooting daggers at me with her eyes. Obviously, if she hadn't heard our conversation firsthand, she's definitely heard about it now, but it doesn't faze me. I'm too excited about the prospect of Connor texting me to even care.

I linger by the door after school, hoping Connor will walk out and talk to me again, but I don't see him. I know I can't delay any longer once Marie starts shouting, "Emma! Let's go! What are you *doing?*"

With a sigh, we start the walk home. Marie is awfully cranky, whining that her feet hurt, and she's hungry, and can't I walk any faster? I ignore her, admiring the leaves starting to grow back on the trees and the little flowers occasionally sprouting up. I pick up a long stick to use as a cane. I feel powerful, like a queen striding out to address the peasants.

"Dude, what is with you?" Marie asks as we turn down our street.

"Dude, what do you mean?"

"You're being really quiet, and you keep humming." She pauses for a second, tilting her head to the side before adding, "And why are you carrying that giant stick?"

I shrug. "I had a good day."

5:12 P.M.

No text from Connor yet.

Mom calls us for dinner. Dad's sitting down as I walk into the kitchen. "Excellent, taco Tuesday!" he says.

Once we're all settled, plates full, Marie says, "Let's play High-Low."

This time, I'm game.

"I'll start," I announce. Mom looks surprised, raising one eyebrow at me. Seriously, who *can't* do that? "What? I had a good day." I put down my taco before I start. "High: We're starting a new project in science. We're building rollercoasters, and I got a really good partner." Even though it's only my family around, I can still feel my cheeks heating up a little. I ignore it and continue, "Low: Ruby had choir after school, so I had to walk home without her."

"Sounds rough," Dad chimes in.

"Who's your partner for the project?" Mom asks. Oh, no. I should have thought this through. Now Mom's going to ask a thousand questions.

"Oh, you don't know him," I try to get away with.

Dad chimes in again, "Him? A boy? Oh, no, it's starting." He puts his hand to his chest like he's having a heart attack.

"Dad, calm down." I roll my eyes at him. Mom is looking at me expectantly.

"Well, that explains the humming," Marie says, looking at Dad like they're in cahoots.

"Humming?" Mom smirks as she scoops some rice onto her plate.

"You guys, stop it. It's nothing." I take another bite from my own plate. "Who's next?" I ask, trying to take the attention off me.

"Nope. Still on you," Mom says. "Who's your partner?"

I sigh before giving in. "Connor." Even as I say it, I can hear the excitement in my voice, and despite every effort to stop it, I'm smiling again.

"Ooooh, Connooooorrrr!" Marie starts making kissy noises. I ball up my napkin and throw it at her. Dad joins in, planting a big fat one on my cheek. I'm slightly embarrassed, but I can't help laughing as I wipe the slobber off my face.

"Okay, okay," Mom says a little too casually. "Who's next?"

"Me!" Marie shouts, raising her fork in the air and unintentionally flinging rice at all of us.

CHAPTER 13

I'm not cool!

TUESDAY, APRIL 27TH
7:09 P.M.
BEDROOM

Still nothing from Connor. Why hasn't he texted? This is driving me crazy. And so is my mother. I can tell she really wants to ask me about Connor. She and Dad were whispering in the kitchen after dinner. I couldn't hear what they were saying, but I know it was about me. I don't know why. Again, it's not like Connor's my boyfriend.

Yet.

Hopefully.

I decide to sit at my desk and doodle in my notebook while I patiently wait. I wonder what Connor is doing? He probably had baseball practice after school. I don't know what time that would go until, though.

Does he actually like me? Am I thinking too much into this? I put my pen down and examine myself in the mirror. I let myself feel hopeful. Why am I overthinking it? Connor asked to be my partner, he smiled at me in the hallway, and he asked for my number—me, boring, flat-chested, Emma.

Speaking of, I look at my chest. My shirt falls straight down. Not even a little anthill. I put my arms at my sides and squeeze my elbows in. Still nothing. Last week I asked Mom to get me one of those "magic" padded-bras that add two cup sizes. She said no.

"Please! It's the perfect solution. Look at me!" I pulled my shirt tightly against my chest. "Nothing!"

Mom was unimpressed. "It's false advertising."

"Why does it matter?" I argued. "No one is going to be touching them!"

Mom sighed as she finished folding a pair of Dad's underwear (gross) and then said, "They'll grow, Emma," and walked out of the room. Easy for her to say! She's got knockers for days.

I huff now the same way I did that day. My door creaks open, and Albus strolls into the room. He hops up on the bed. I close my notebook and plop down next to him. He's feeling snuggly, so I pet his furry little belly. But he changes his mind quickly and swats at my hand. I ignore it and reach for another belly scratch. As he captures my hand between his paws, my phone buzzes. My heart jumps into my throat.

"Ow!" Albus rolls over and sprints out of the room after his attack on my hand. I leap for my phone, afraid to actually look at it. I squeeze my eyes shut and silently pray, *Please, oh, please, let this be Connor.* I open my eyes, and my heart plummets back down into my chest. It's Ruby.

7:12 P.M.

Ruby was checking in to see if Connor had texted. She was as disappointed and confused as me. Cher piped in not to worry about it because sometimes boys will wait to text so they don't seem too eager.

How does she know all this stuff? She's only had one boyfriend. But I guess it's one more than I've had.

7:14 P.M.

Still. That's stupid. He doesn't need to play it cool. I'm not cool!

7:18 P.M.

I am getting very antsy. It feels like my body is wound up very tightly, and every little thing is annoying me. I yelled at Marie for walking too loudly in the hallway. She stuck her tongue out in response. Oi vey.

What if he doesn't text me? What if we're wrong? What if he doesn't like me?

7:21 P.M.

Mom is lurking outside my bedroom. She keeps walking by, pretending to do things. I know she wants to come in here and talk about Connor. She knows I like him. Ugh, why did I have to tell her everything the day of the zit?

7:23 P.M.

She's walked by four times in the last two minutes. I counted.

I give in when she *casually* walks by with the same basket of laundry I've seen twice already.

"Mom, why don't you just come in here?"

She pops her head around the door. "What do you mean? I'm getting stuff done." I raise (both) my eyebrows at her. She laughs and sighs. "Okay, you caught me." She sits on the corner of my bed. I'm cross-legged at the top, pretending to do homework. "What are you up to?" she asks, flipping over the textbook next to me. "Math?"

"Yeah, sort of. Math is the worst." I shut the book and put it on my nightstand. "So..." I fold my hands in my lap, waiting.

"Soooo... what?" She shakes her head slightly.

"What do you want to know?" I slump my shoulders and look down at her. Something catches my attention. "Hey!" I shout, pointing at her face.

"What?" She touches her cheek, "Is there something on my face?"

"No..." I'm staring, but I can't help it.

"What is your deal?"

"We have the same eyes," I tell her slowly.

"Yeah, goofball. I know that." She taps my knee.

"They're so pretty."

"I know." She smiles and bats her eyelashes. We both giggle. My phone buzzes. Once again, I freeze, and the drummers start practicing in my chest again. Mom notices. "Is this the boy texting you?"

"I don't know. Maybe." I pause, still not picking the phone up. "I hope so," I admit, biting my lip. Mom and her sea-glass eyes stare back at me. How have I never noticed that before?

She picks up my phone. "No name." She turns the screen toward me.

I snatch the phone. It's Connor. It's got to be. Who else would be texting me from a number I don't know? Oh my God. Oh my God. Oh my God. My cheeks are burning, my hands are shaking, and my heart is thumping in my chest.

Mom laughs and gets up. "Calm down, sweetie. It's just a text." She puts her hands on my shoulders and gently pushes me back to sit on the bed. I didn't even realize I stood up.

She moves some hair behind my ear and says, "I'll let you have some privacy. But we're not done talking. Okay?" I nod. She pauses at the door. "Em?" I tear my eyes away from the message notification. "Remember: Boys come and go, but you'll always be you. You're number one." And she turns and walks out.

That was weird. I open the message from Connor.

Connor: Hey, Emma, it's Connor.

I'm a little disappointed. I mean, I don't know what I was hoping for. A big long paragraph professing his love for me, asking me to be his girlfriend? Actually, yes, that would have been ideal. On the bright side, this is easy enough to respond to.

Me: Hey, what's up?

I hit send before I can think too much into it. I wait patiently for a reply.

7:27 P.M.
Why hasn't he replied?

7:30 P.M.
Connor texted back. Must focus.

7:42 P.M.
This conversation is pretty boring. He had baseball practice today. He ate pasta for dinner. He's watching TV now. I thought talking to boys on the phone was much more of a thrill ride. Stupid romantic comedies, once again setting my expectations too high.

Connor: Soooo… I'm glad you wanted to be my partner on this rollercoaster project.

Ahhhh! Now this is what I'm talking about. I smile down at the screen, pondering what to send back.

Me: Me too :)

Ugh, I wish Ruby and Cher were here to help me. Cher would probably come up with a response that's sassy yet wouldn't sound like I'm trying too hard. I sort of want to ask him why he turned Audrey down. No way. I'm too chicken.

7:43 P.M.

Me: So, kind of a weird question, but why didn't you want to be Audrey's partner?

Oh my God! I can't believe I sent that. My heart is beating so fast. I feel like I ran a mile. Ruby and Cher are going to die when I tell them about this.

7:46 P.M.
This was a bad idea. He isn't responding. Oh, poooo. What have I done? Now I've messed everything up over a stupid question. Ugggghhhh, Emma, you're an idiot.

I throw myself onto the bed and bang my head against the wall. I cry out in pain. Mom calls up to make sure I'm okay. Physically? Yes. Mentally? No.

7:49 P.M.
My phone buzzes. I sit up, still rubbing the place I hit my head. I'm too scared to open it. What if he's like, *That's not really any of your business. And I think maybe we shouldn't work together anymore.* Or what if he says, *Wow, that's a rude question. I can't be your partner.* I groan. But the urge overwhelms me. I have to know what he said. I open the message.

I smile.

Connor: Because she's a jerk. Eye-roll emoji.

I kiss my phone and *carefully* lie back on my bed to respond.

Me: Well, yeah, I know that, haha. Thought you
guys were close, though.

I pause before I hit send. Whatever, I've already committed to this conversation.
Connor texts back almost immediately.

Connor: Nah, she just wants people to think that.

This is seriously the best day of my life. Possibly of all mankind. Not only does Connor want to be my partner and maybe like me, but he also clearly does not like Audrey. I hop off the bed again and dance around my room, humming a random tune. I don't care if anyone sees me.

9:47 P.M.
BED
Connor and I talk for the rest of the night. After my Audrey questions, he was like...

Connor: Let's talk about something else. Audrey's
pretty boring. ;)

We talked about school, teachers, friends, TV shows— everything. I had no idea we had so much in common. He must like me. Right? *Two hours* of texting?

Connor: Sweet dreams, cutie.

I can't even respond. It's too perfect. I reread our messages from the last two hours. I'm smiling from ear to ear. I squeal and pull my covers over my head, kicking my legs. I cannot physically contain the euphoria I am feeling.

I'm going to have a boyfriend!

10:32 P.M.

I can't fall asleep. I can't stop thinking about Connor. He is so dreamy. His wavy, dark brown hair is long enough that he can run his hands through it, but it's also not *too* long. It's always a little messed up, but like it's on purpose.

Oh, and his eyes, his baby blue eyes. They're like a fresh piece of peppermint gum—the perfect kind of blue. No, that's weird. They're like... ice—ice-blue is a thing, isn't it?

If we end up going out, and falling in love, and then dating through high school and college, and then getting married and having kids, I hope our children have his eyes.

Am I insane?

10:59 P.M.

Why am I still awake? I have to get up early, so I can put on my sea-glass eye makeup.

11:09 P.M.

I'll try counting... 1... 2... 3... 4... 5... 6... 7... 8... 9... 10... 11...

11:11 P.M.

It's 11:11. Make a wish. I wish Connor was my boyfriend.

11:13 P.M.

Oh, shoot, what number was I on? I give up. It wasn't working anyway. I flip my pillow to the other side and roll over to get more comfortable. I squeeze my eyes shut, willing myself to fall asleep.

11:25 P.M.

Didn't work. I think about Connor again... Connor and I walk down the hallway, holding hands. He looks at me lovingly with his beautiful, ice-blue eyes. Audrey frowns at us from her locker, jealous of our love. I wave to Ruby and Cher, who smile and say, "Aww, aren't they the cutest couple ever?" I look up at my boyfriend, and he smiles back at me...

CHAPTER 14

See you in science.

WEDNESDAY, APRIL 28TH
6:45 A.M.

My alarm blares in my ear. I groan and roll over to snooze it until I remember—Connor. My partner. I hop out of bed and sprint into the bathroom to start getting ready.

6:46 A.M.
BATHROOM

Noooo!

I have a zit on my nose. In the same spot as before. This *can't* be happening. Why me? I sit down on the toilet and start crying. I know it's stupid, but I feel like my head is going to explode if I don't let it out. I don't know what else to do. I put my face in my hands and wail. Mom comes flying into the bathroom.

"Emma, what on earth is wrong?" She crouches down to my level.

I can't summon any words. I point to my nose. The reality of my ugliness hits me, and I cover my face again.

"Oh, honey, that's nothing. We can cover it right up. Take a hot shower. It'll help with the swelling."

I sniffle and peek up at her. "Are you sure?"

"Positive." She stands up, pulling me by the arms. "Up. Shower. Let's go!"

8:01 A.M.
IN THE CAR

Mom was able to cover up the zit, thank God. But with the extra time spent getting ready, I didn't have time to walk to school with Ruby. On the bright side, Mom not only helped me cover up the zit, but she also helped me do my eyeliner for my sea-glass eyes!

"Only because it's subtle, though," she told me. "You don't need to wear a lot of makeup. You're naturally beautiful. And smart," she added, pointing the eyeliner at me. I rolled my sea-glass eyes at her.

And even though we're running late and I have a zit on my nose, I actually feel kind of great. I blow-dried my hair, and I have my sea-glass eye makeup on. I am totally going to wow Connor when I see him.

"Why are you so dressed up?" Marie asks from the front seat. That's a tell-tale sign I was running late—Marie beat me to the car.

"What are you talking about? I'm wearing my uniform." I casually flip my hair behind my shoulder.

"No, like, your face," she says. "It's weird." She frowns and turns back to the front.

Oh, no. Do I look like I tried too hard? My shoulders slump. Trying too hard to look pretty is not cool. You want to look pretty like it's without trying, like it's easy. Even though it isn't. What's the deal with that?

"You look great, Em," Mom says as she buckles her seat belt. She winks at me in the rearview mirror. I can also see myself in the mirror, and I do look pretty. My eyes look bigger than usual, and I can see their sea-glassiness from my spot in the back. I sit up taller.

"Let's go. We're going to be late," I say impatiently.

8:13 A.M.
HALLWAY

"Oh my God, Emma, no wonder you were late!" Ruby exclaims as she strides over to Cher and me at our lockers. "You look amazing! Give me a twirl!" I can't help it; even though I know I'll look ridiculous, I give Ruby a twirl and blow her a kiss at the end. "Yas, girl!" she says, high-fiving me.

I laugh and turn to Cher, expecting her to say something, too. She looks me up and down. "Yeah, for sure." She gives me a forced smile. "Listen, I have to go talk to Mr. White about my math grade before first period. I'll see you guys in class." Before Ruby or I can say anything, she's walking quickly down the hall. She looks back and gives us a half-wave with another forced smile.

"What is her deal?" I ask Ruby. "Was something wrong this morning?"

Ruby glances at Cher's receding figure. "I don't know. She was talking to Audrey again when I got here," she says darkly.

What? Why would she be talking to Audrey? That makes no sense. Ruby must be thinking the same thing because she says, "I know," and purses her lips. I want to talk more about this, but Connor walks up right at that moment.

"Hey, Emma." He pauses, taking in my appearance. "Wow, you look... different."

"What does different mean?" Ruby interjects. "Like, she looks good? Because she does!"

I elbow Ruby discreetly as Connor stutters, "Oh, uh, yeah, of course." He smiles nervously at Ruby, who's giving him a skeptical once-over. He turns back to me and says, "Can I walk you to class?"

"Definitely." I smile shyly. I hug my books to my chest. I think I'm doing okay, even though I can feel the heat creeping into my cheeks.

"Okay, but I'm going to the same place," Ruby says, poking her head over my shoulder. "Can I come, too?"

I groan. "Oh my God, Ruby!" Sometimes I want to punch her. The smile on her face falters, and her eyes dart between Connor and me a few times. A small knot forms in my stomach.

Luckily, Connor doesn't skip a beat. He laughs and says, "Definitely."

Ruby's smile returns, and the three of us make our way to English, Ruby to my left and Connor to my right. He doesn't say anything as we walk down the hallway, but once we're in the classroom, he turns and says, "See you in science." Then with a wave, he goes to his seat at the opposite side of the room. Ruby gives me a small hip-bump before heading to her seat.

8:44 A.M.
ENGLISH

Ms. Stein is blabbering on about sentence structure, and I cannot focus. So many thoughts are running through my brain—too many to think about when I need to use a comma in a complex sentence.

What did Connor mean when he said, "See you in science?" We're in the same class right now. I can literally see him from my seat. I'll probably see him on the walk there, too. What a weird thing to say.

And what is going on with Cher? She walked in after the bell rang with a pass from Mr. White, and she smiled that odd, forced smile at me again as she passed my desk. It's making me feel weird, like my stomach feels nervous, but it doesn't know why.

I wonder how my hair is holding up. Does it still look good? What about my makeup? Mom said the concealer should last all day, but what if I have an itch? I tenderly touch the bridge of my nose. Everything feels fine. Maybe I should go to the bathroom to check on it.

"Yes, Emma?"

"Can I go to the washroom?"

"Right now? Right now is the moment you're going to ask that question?" Ms. Stein says.

"Um, no?"

"That's what I thought. So, if the sentence starts with an independent clause..."

Ugh. She's so irritating. If I become a teacher, I'll remember what it's like to be a teenager and worry about how you look. I will always let people go to the bathroom when they ask.

9:10 A.M.

From somewhere far away, I hear Ms. Stein ask for volunteers. I focus my attention back on what she's saying. "Come on, friends. I need three more people to come up and be part of my sentence." Nope. Not happening. Connor shrugs his shoulders and lifts his hand up off his desk. Hunter lets out a big laugh.

"Thank you, Connor." Ms. Stein gives Hunter an icy stare. "How about you, Mr. Schmidt? Care to join us up here?" Hunter makes a show of dragging himself out of his seat and up to the front of the room. A couple of people laugh, including me, but Ms. Stein is merely happy to have another volunteer. She smiles out at the rest of the class. "One more?" She scans the room and notices a hand. "Audrey, what a surprise!" I snicker at Ms. Stein's comment. Audrey is horrible at English.

"My pleasure, Ms. Stein," Audrey drawls. I swear I see a flicker of an eye-roll on Ms. Stein's face. Ha! Even she doesn't like Audrey. I'm appreciating this moment when out of nowhere, all of my stuff is knocked to the floor—pens, note-books, papers, it all goes flying. Audrey turns back as she continues walking to the front of the room; she looks right at me and scratches her nose.

My blood is boiling. I lean over to start gathering my papers, and Alejandra comes around to help me. "She's horrible," she whispers.

Back in my seat, I see that Audrey has wiggled her way between Connor and Hunter. She's smirking at me as she runs her fingers through her hair. I can hear my angry blood gurgling in my brain. I hate her. For the first time ever, I wish I had volunteered to go up to the front of the room.

Ms. Stein starts explaining what they're doing up there—something about rearranging themselves so the sentence is correctly written—but I'm watching Audrey (the period of the sentence), who is watching Connor (the comma), who seems oblivious to all of this and is actually trying to figure out where he needs to go.

See you in science, I doodle in my notebook.

CHAPTER 15

I like to build things.

WEDNESDAY, APRIL 28TH
9:15 A.M.

I get so lost in my doodling I jump a little when the bell rings. Alejandra laughs behind me, and Ms. Stein says, "Oh, darn." She looks at the clock behind her. "Okay, well, we'll continue with this tomorrow. Have a good day. I'll see you later—wait! I need those cards back!" She dashes around the room, grabbing the cards from the volunteers before they leave.

I grab my stuff and head toward the door. I casually check to see if Connor left already. He did. I'm a little bummed. I thought (hoped) he might want to walk to science together, too. But at least this way I have a chance to talk to Cher.

Ruby is waiting outside Ms. Stein's room. "Where's Cher?" I ask.

Ruby frowns. "I thought she was still in there." She pokes her head back into Ms. Stein's room. She walks out and shrugs. Further down the hallway, I see Cher's blond ponytail swinging from side to side.

"Cher!" I call out. She doesn't hear me. "*Cher!*" I call louder. She hears me this time and turns around. She hesitates for half a second, glancing over her shoulder, and then waits for us to catch up to her.

Ruby cuts right to the chase. "What is going on with you?"

"Nothing," she snaps. She looks down, biting her lip. She sighs as if giving in. "I'm just having a bad day." When she looks up at us, her green eyes are welling up. Ruby immediately goes to Cher's side to give her a hug. It's a little difficult with our piles of books. It's more like the awkward side hug you give to someone you don't really want to hug, but Ruby means it. She's a great hugger.

"What happened?" Ruby's dark eyebrows knit together with concern.

Cher takes a deep breath and shakes her head. "I don't really want to talk about it right now." Ruby and I nod, and we start walking toward science. Cher sniffs, and Ruby puts her arm around Cher's shoulder.

"We love you," she tells Cher. I hip-bump her from the other side.

She sniffs again and quietly says, "I know."

9:20 A.M.
SCIENCE

I'm still thinking about Cher as we work on our bellringer. What is going on? Is it something with her family? She rarely talks about the divorce these days, but that doesn't mean she couldn't be upset about it from time to time. Ruby gets upset about her dad, and he died a long time ago. Or could Cher be that worried about her math grade? No way, Cher does really well in school—like straight A's well. Could it be me? She's been acting strange since all this Connor stuff started.

With all the drama in the hallway, I almost forgot what being in science means—Connor. Mrs. Short gives us directions and what we should "aim to accomplish." Why can't teachers say, "Get this done or you lose points?" That would make a lot more sense.

"Alright, start tinkering, my little engineers," Mrs. Short tells us. As people start moving to go sit with their partners, she attempts to shout over the noise, "And let me know if you have questions! That's why I'm here!"

"Good luck!" Ruby squeals.

I smile but then get serious. "You too. Let me know if you get any information out of her." We both look back at Cher, who's clearing space for Ruby to join her.

"Will do." She starts gathering her stuff.

Connor walks over, confident and adorable, as always. "Hey," he says. He's soooo cool. How can he possibly like me? Ruby heads back to Cher's table, leaving me alone with the coolest boy in our class. And he wanted to be *my* partner. I smile and gesture for him to sit down. My heart starts whirring.

"So, any ideas for this rollercoaster?" I ask.

Be cool, Emma, I remind myself.

"Um, actually, I do have a couple," he tells me sheepishly. He rubs the back of his neck.

"Oh." I'm surprised by this. I didn't think Connor was super into school. He's not like Hunter, who seems to barely scrape by, but he never seems enthused by anything we do.

He taps his pen against his notebook. "I like to build things."

"That's really cool." I read in a magazine once that you should touch a guy's arm to let him know you like what he's saying. I do that. I don't know if I do it right, though, because

Connor looks down at my hand on his arm. I quickly pull it back. Stupid idea. My cheeks burst into flame.

Connor keeps talking like he didn't notice my idiotic arm touch. "Yeah, I used to build things with Legos all the time when I was little."

My heart starts whirring more quickly. "Really? So did I." Connor's ice-blue eyes light up. "I mean, don't get too excited. I mostly made houses for the little people to live in."

Connor laughs, which oddly sounds like popcorn popping. Or a robot. I add my own nervous giggle, which sounds like a squirrel, so I'm not one to talk.

Mrs. Short's voice breaks through our laughter, "I hear a lot of talking, but not much of it is about rollercoasters, people. Let's get going!"

Connor smirks. "C'mon." He reaches over and flips my notebook open. "Let's start planning."

LUNCH

I come flying into the lunchroom, a big, goofy smile plastered on my face. I slide into my seat across from Cher and next to Ruby. Cher still looks a little down. She's gazing out at the rest of the lunchroom and fiddling with a napkin. I wonder if Ruby got anything out of her in science. I glance to my left, but Ruby is too busy twisting open her Oreo to notice.

"Guys," I say.

"Emma," Ruby retorts.

Cher turns back to the table and pops a grape in her mouth.

"Connor invited me to a party Saturday night!" I announce. "Well, us really, he said we should all come!" I start frantically clapping my hands and making a strange, high-pitched noise I did not know I was capable of.

"Yes!" Ruby does a fist pump into the air. "Where is it?"

"At his house. His birthday is next week, but his family is going out of town for a wedding, so he's having the party early." I am bursting with excitement. I can't sit still. "Cher? You in?"

"For sure," she says with a smile—a real Cher-smile with her perfect white teeth, not the forced, pained smile she was giving this morning.

This makes me happy. I throw my hands in the air with a "Woo!" Ruby laughs and does the same. We both look at Cher expectantly.

She rolls her eyes but throws her hands up with a "Woo," a little less enthusiastically than Ruby and I did. I smile and clap my hands again.

3:11 P.M.
WALKING HOME

As soon as we're far enough from school that I know we're safe, I ask Ruby, "So, did you find out what's going on with Cher?"

"What's wrong with Cher?" Marie asks from behind us. She tries to walk next to Ruby, but there isn't room for all three of us on the sidewalk.

"None of your business." I speed up my walking a little.

"Come on," she begs, matching my speed. "Tell me. Pleeeease?"

"No. You're being annoying."

"Emma," Ruby scolds me, "be nice." Ruby doesn't get it. She's an only child, so she doesn't know how irritating little sisters are.

I ignore Ruby. "Seriously, Marie, we need to talk. Privately." I push her ahead of us. She doesn't fight it, but only because I know her plan: She's going to walk slowly and quietly listen. But it's not worth trying to stop her; there's no privacy when we're walking home.

"Okay," I say, now that Marie is at least pretending not to be part of our conversation. "What did she say?"

"Honestly, nothing, really." Ruby shrugs and pushes her braids behind her ears. I wait patiently for more information. "All she said was that she had stuff going on at home, that it was nothing to worry about, and could we please not talk about it anymore. Then she acted normal. A little mean, but I think that's pretty much normal."

I think this over for a second. "Well, okay. If she doesn't want to talk about it, we can't force her to."

"That's kind of what I thought," Ruby says.

Now I shrug my shoulders. "Okay." We leave it at that.

Ruby reaches her arms forward and tickles Marie. Marie shrieks with laughter and flails about, trying to escape Ruby's grasp. They both run off ahead of me.

7:40 P.M.
Mom asked a thousand questions about Connor's party on Saturday. *Whose party is it? What time does it start? Are his parents going to be home? Are Ruby and Cher going with you? How are you going to get there? How are you going to get home? What time are you going to be home?*

Dad's only input was, "Don't kiss any boys."

I grit my teeth and make it through the interrogation, and as a result, I get to go! Yessss! I text Ruby and Cher to let them know. Ruby responds with about fifty partyhorn emojis.

Cher: Me too! Should we have a sleepover?

Me: Definitely.

Cher: How about your house?

Ruby: Yes! Maybe Emma's dad will get us burri-
tos again!!

Me: Haha okay. I'll ask.

After the party questioning, though, the sleepover was a
no-brainer. We are a *go* for the most amazing night *ever!* I'm
pretty sure Connor is going to ask me out on Saturday. He
was totally flirting with me today, and then after class, he
said, "I'm really glad you're my partner, Emma," and gave me
a high five!

I'm going to have a boyfriend!

CHAPTER 16

Are my lips kissable?

THURSDAY, APRIL 28TH
7:41 A.M.

Ruby is quiet this morning. I could tell she wasn't feeling like herself as soon she walked out the door. She was missing the unmistakable pep that she always has in her step.

"What's wrong, Rubs?" I ask immediately.

She shrugs, her brown eyes down on the ground. She gets like this sometimes. Quiet and sad.

"Is it your dad?" I ask gently.

She shrugs again. After a couple of seconds, she says, "Today's his birthday."

I put my arm around her. "I love you."

She lifts her head slightly and gives me a small smile. "I know."

"Do you want to talk about it?"

She looks up at the sky for a second. "No," she says quietly.

We walk to school without talking anymore. It makes my heart hurt when she's like this. I can't imagine how she feels. Mom says I just need to be there for her and let her talk about her dad when she wants to. She'll casually mention him from time to time but doesn't tell a lot of stories about him. I never met him. He died only a few months before Ruby and I met in kindergarten.

Life isn't fair.

3:15 P.M.
WALKING HOME

Marie skips ahead of us as we walk home. Ruby's still quiet. She was quiet most of the day.

"It sucks," she says out of nowhere.

"What does?" Ruby looks at me like I've lost my mind. "Oh my God, your dad! I'm so sorry!"

Ruby lets out a small laugh. "It's okay, Em. I'm okay. It's just... hard, you know?"

I nod, staying quiet in case she wants to talk some more.

"He would love a day like today. The sun is shining, the air is crisp, it's finally starting to warm up a little." She turns her face up to feel the warmth of the sun. She sighs. "Mom always says life is too short. 'I know that all too well, baby,'" she says, imitating Georgia.

I don't know what to say.

Ruby shrugs. "No point in moping all day. Right? My dad would want me to enjoy the sunshine, to be happy."

"I think so," I say. "Do you want a hug?"

She stops and turns to face me. "Yeah. Thanks, Emma."

"For what?"

"For being there for me. Always."

"Always." I pull her into a tight hug.

8:22 P.M.

I gave my dad a hug when he got home today. I think he was surprised, but he didn't say anything. He just rubbed my back.

FRIDAY, APRIL 29TH
7:40 A.M.

Ruby is definitely feeling better. She comes flying out the door this morning.

"Emma! You have to hear about this dream I had last night! This weekend is going to be *epic*. I can feel it."

4:02 P.M.

School was torturous today. It went on for about a thousand years. Except science, of course, which went by so fast. I'm barely even nervous around Connor anymore. Well, except every time he walks over, and every time we make eye contact, and—okay, maybe I'm still nervous around him. And I know I'm always a little pink when we leave class because Cher tells me. Every. Day.

"Your cheeks are red again," she said today.

I touched them. It's not like I can control it. "I know," was all I said.

7:12 P.M.
BEDROOM

I wonder if Connor will kiss me when he asks me to be his girlfriend. I've never kissed a boy. Am I going to get my first boyfriend *and* my first kiss tomorrow?

Cher kissed a boy at camp last summer. She said it was after the bonfire, under the stars. It sounded *so* romantic, like something out of a movie. They texted back and forth for a couple of weeks after camp, but it was too hard to do long-distance.

Like me, Ruby hasn't kissed any boys. Whenever we talk about kissing, she brushes it off and says something like, "Boys are a waste of time. I'm an independent woman."

My heart is racing even thinking about kissing Connor. I was admiring his lips in science today; they're plump, and they look soft and very kissable. Are my lips kissable?

I run over to the mirror to investigate. My lips are pretty average. A little on the thin side, but definitely a distinct lip on both the top and bottom. They're not overly chapped. I lick them. But they also don't feel very soft. I run my finger over my bottom lip. Nope, not soft enough. I open my desk drawer and search for a ChapStick. Once I find it, I lather it on. I decide to do this as often as I can between now and the party. I make a kissy face at myself in the mirror. That needs work, too.

7:20 P.M.

I wonder if Mom would let me out of the house wearing lipstick tomorrow. She doesn't like it when I go overboard on makeup. I tried to wear mascara to school once, and she made me get out of the car, go back inside, and wash it off before we could leave. I was so mad. We were going to be late as it was, and I had spent *forever* trying not to poke myself in the eye.

She's more lenient now—especially if it's a "natural" look like my sea-glass eyes, but I don't know how she'd feel about lipstick.

7:26 P.M.

I stole one of Mom's lipsticks to practice with. It's a soft pink, and it makes my lips way more kissable. I hide it in my drawer. I'm wearing this tomorrow. To be safe, I'll put it on after I leave.

8:41 P.M.

I want to go to bed early, so I'm well-rested for the party, but I don't feel even a teensy bit tired. I keep thinking about the party, imagining scenarios, all of which end with Connor kissing me and asking me to be his girlfriend and everyone cheering in the background.

8:42 P.M.
And Audrey standing on the sideline, crying, full of remorse for all the mean things she's done to me.

CHAPTER 17

There are no boyfriends!

SATURDAY, MAY 1ST
6:02 A.M.

It's party day!

I groan when I realize how early it is. Twelve hours until the party. Well, eleven hours and fifty-eight minutes, technically. What am I going to do with myself?

8:34 A.M.

Excellent, I fell back asleep. Now it's only nine hours and twenty-six minutes until the party. That's still a lot of time to fill. I text Ruby and Cher.

Me: OMG. SO. EXCITED. FOR TONIGHT!! Want to come over and get ready together?

Ruby: YAS! Of course! What time?

Me: Hmmm… Party starts at 6, but we don't wanna be too early, ya know? Soooo we should get there at like 6:10? Start getting ready around 5? Does that sound right?

Ruby: Girl, I have no idea…

Cher: Why are you two always up so early? Between my phone buzzing and my brother screaming, I guess I'm not getting any more sleep. -_-

Ruby: Aww, don't be a cranky-pants, Cher! Tonight's going to be so fun!

Cher: True. 5 sounds good to me.

Me: Yayy!! I'll have my mom make some snacks. CANNOT WAIT!!

8:38 A.M.
KITCHEN

I'm eating some toast when Mom comes in to refill her coffee. She sits down with me, swirling the milky liquid with a spoon. The clinking of the spoon against the mug is a morning staple.

"You excited for tonight?" she asks with a smile. I nod, trying to be nonchalant. Mom nods, too. "So..."

I know that "so." She wants to have some sort of *talk*. I give her a sidelong glance and hold my breath, waiting for it.

"Is Connor going to be your boyfriend?" She leans toward me like we're in on a secret together.

"Oh my God, Mom! Come on."

"You come on. I'm your mother. I can ask these questions."

"No, you can't. It's embarrassing."

"You know, I was your age once, too." She reaches for my hand. "I remember what it was like to have a crush on a boy. The rush of adrenaline, thinking about being near him, your heart pounding... Sound familiar?" I smile despite myself. "Thought so," Mom says with an air of satisfaction. "So, come on. Tell me." She lets go of my hand and lightly slaps it like Ruby does sometimes.

"It's not that big of a deal, Mom." (Yes, it is.)

"Yes, it is. You'll never forget your first boyfriend, Emma. I had my first boyfriend in eighth grade. His name was Calvin, and he bought me a little stuffed animal on Valentine's Day. Then he was really mean to me when we broke up." Mom is thoughtful for a second and then chuckles. "Turns out he's gay. I ran into him in college once, and we had a good laugh at ourselves."

I take a bite of my toast. "I thought this conversation was supposed to be about me?"

"Don't talk with food in your mouth. And you're right. Tell me the gossip." She puts her chin in her hand.

"There's not much to tell..." I press my finger onto some toast crumbs, stalling, but Mom is waiting patiently. I sigh, giving in. I tell her about how much I like Connor, how cute he is, and that we're partners in science and have so much in common. "So... I don't know... I mean, I'm hoping..." I'm stumbling for the right words.

Mom sighs. "You're so cute, Emma. You're blushing."

I put my hands against my cheeks and huff. I knew she wouldn't understand. "It is *not* cute. It's totally humiliating, and it happens every time I talk to Connor."

"Okay, okay." Mom puts her hands up in an 'I surrender' stance. "I get it, trust me." She puts her hands down and grimaces. "I'm sorry, sweetie, but you inherited that from me."

"Thanks," I say sarcastically.

"Can I be Mom-like for a minute, Em?"

"Is there any stopping you?" She shakes her head, smiling. I groan. "Go ahead."

"When you go to this party tonight, I want you to remember that no matter what happens, being someone's girlfriend does not define you." She grabs my hand again and squeezes it tightly. "And you don't have to do *anything* with *anyone* that you don't want to."

I know my face is as red as a tomato now. "Mom!" I pull my hand from her grasp. "What do you think I'm going to be doing?"

"I want you to be smart and take care of yourself, Emma. That's all."

This conversation needs to end, like two minutes ago. "I will, Mom. Promise." I put my fingers up in the Girl Scout salute.

Marie chooses this moment to walk in. "Promise what?"

"Nothing." I take the last bite of my toast and stand up to take my plate to the sink.

"To tell us about her new boyfriend tomorrow," Mom fake whispers to Marie.

"Seriously, Mom?"

Marie perks up. "Who's your boyfriend?"

"No one."

Then, because I'm that lucky, Dad walks in. "Who has a boyfriend?" He points, dragging his finger back and forth across the three of us. "No boyfriends."

"There are no boyfriends! Mom is making stuff up." I turn my back to them as I rinse my plate. I hear them whispering and giggling. "Okay, I'm going up to my room. No one follow me. Mom, will you make some snacks for later? Ruby and Cher are coming over at five, so we can all get ready together."

She nods, pretending to feel sorry for spilling the beans, but I see her raise her eyebrows at Dad. I turn to Dad and raise my hands in the same surrender-pose Mom used before.

"No boyfriend," I say, and then I run up the stairs.

9:11 A.M.
BEDROOM
My family is so nosy.

4:55 P.M.
The doorbell rings, and I go flying down the stairs. It's Ruby. She has two giant bags with her. Dad toddles up behind me.

"Geez, Ruby. Are you moving in?" he says.

"Oh, Mr. Bishop, you're so funny." She laughs and waves her hand at him dismissively. "These are all my beautifying supplies. And four outfit options."

"Obviously," I say.

"Teenage girls are strange." Dad sighs, plopping himself on the couch.

Ruby comes in the door, and I take one of the bags from her.

"Okay, seriously, how much did you bring with you?" I groan as I pull the bag up over my shoulder.

"Only the essentials. My mom let me bring the good makeup too," she says excitedly.

"Oooh, really? Yay!" I squeal as we run up the stairs.

4:58 P.M.
As Ruby and I lay out our clothing options, Cher walks into my bedroom.

"When did you get here?" I ask her. "I didn't hear the doorbell."

"No," she says, a little exasperated. "I texted you guys when I was a block away, but you didn't respond."

"Oh, sorry. We were preparing," Ruby says, showcasing our work thus far.

"It's okay." Cher drops her bag on the floor to take her jacket off. "Your dad was walking out as I was getting out of the car."

I clap to focus our attention on the task at hand. "Okay, ladies. Let's prettify!"

5:55 P.M.

After about an hour of outfit changing, makeup applying (and taking off and reapplying), and hair straightening, curling, and styling, we are looking pretty fab. Ruby admires herself in the full-length mirror on the back of my door. She poses with her hands on her hips, turns around and pops a knee, and winks at her reflection.

"I look amazing," she says, turning back to us. She has new skinny braids like her mom, and she put them half up with a little bun on top. She's wearing a jean jacket over a black crop top and a high-waisted, white-and-black-patterned skirt. Mom would never let me wear a crop top.

Cher put my hair in a sock bun, so it's all pulled back except for a few wisps here and there. "For texture," Cher said. I decided to wear a white t-shirt dress with my black Converse and to accessorize: hoop earrings and a long necklace with an elephant at the end.

"My mom loves elephants," Ruby said when she noticed my new necklace. I acted surprised, even though I immediately thought of Georgia when I saw it.

Cher is wearing a gray-and-white long-sleeved top tucked into a soft pink flare skirt that is a teensy bit too short and brown booties. Her hair is curled and hair-sprayed within an inch of its life.

"You look great, Ruby. We all do." I smile.

Ruby fans herself. "Stop it, you're making me blush."

"No, that would be Emma." Cher laughs from where she's perched on my bed.

"Not cool, Cher." Ruby furrows her eyebrows. I don't say anything because Cher's right. As soon as the words are out of her mouth, my cheeks warm. I turn away from both of them and look at myself in the mirror.

I see a little pink creeping through my makeup. "You guys, what if I get all red when I'm talking to Connor tonight?"

"I mean, you probably will," Cher says without even looking up from her phone.

What is with Cher? She's had an attitude since she got here. Despite knowing this, my eyes sting. I blink a couple times to stop it. Ruby changes the subject.

"Let's take a couple of pictures before we go." She motions for us to stand up. "Come on. Get up, you lazy farts." We stand up and take a few selfies, all of which I hate.

"Why do I look so weird in pictures? It's like my face gets warped in the camera," I complain.

"I think you look adorable, Em," Ruby says.

I sigh. "Let's have my mom take a couple for us."

"Good idea," Cher says. "Then we can get our whole outfits in."

"*Mom!*" I call from my bedroom door.

"What?" she shouts from the living room.

"Can you come up here?" I hear her get up off the couch and start up the stairs. She peeks her head in the door.

"What do you need?" She takes some pictures of us—standing, sitting, silly, candid—until she says, "Okay, I think you have to like at least one of these. Plus, isn't it time to go?"

My heart starts pounding.

Ruby loops her arm through mine. "Let's do this."

6:11 P.M.
IN THE CAR
OUTSIDE CONNOR'S HOUSE

"I'll pick you up at nine," Mom says, unlocking the doors.

"How about 9:30?" I plead. Mom stares back blankly. "Please?" I turn and raise my eyebrows at Ruby and Cher in the back seat.

"Pleeeease?" they chime in.

Mom sighs. "Fine. 9:30. On the dot, Emma." We all cheer as we hop out of the car.

Mom rolls down the window. "Have fun, girls. Be safe." She gives me a meaningful look. I wave in response.

6:12 P.M.

AT CONNOR'S DOOR

My heart is thumping hard and fast in my chest. "I kind of feel like I'm going to throw up."

Ruby squeezes my hand. "You can do it." Then she lightly hip-bumps me. Cher does the same from the other side.

The door starts to open. I close my eyes and swallow the lump in my throat. When I open them, Connor is standing there.

"Hey," he says with a smile. I swear my heart skips a beat.

CHAPTER 18

Was that a yes?

Connor's house is so cool. He has the whole basement to himself since his brother went to college. Music videos are playing on the TV, and there's a table with bowls of chips, three giant pizzas, and pop. Everyone is hanging out on the couches, which are moved together to form a half-circle.

"Grab a drink and make yourselves comfortable, ladies," Connor says, gesturing around the room. "Emma, what kind of pop do you want?"

How red are my cheeks right now? They feel like they're on fire, and my heart has not slowed down its constant thumping.

"Sprite would be great," I tell Connor. I think I'm playing it pretty cool until I reach out for the cup and notice my hands are shaking. I quickly grab the drink from Connor and turn to the girls. "Let's go find a spot." Connor runs up the stairs to answer the door as we shuffle away.

7:07 P.M.

Basically everyone from our class is here, with a few exceptions: no Laney Lindt or Alejandra. Of course, Audrey and Zoe are here. Audrey's wearing a black skirt that barely covers her butt, and she's laughing obnoxiously loud at everything Hunter says. Zoe has on basically the same outfit as Audrey, but her skirt is noticeably longer, and her t-shirt is blue rather than pink like Audrey's. Audrey keeps looking around to see if Connor is watching her. He's not. He's standing by the food table, eating a piece of pizza and talking to a couple of guys from the baseball team.

Cher, Ruby, and I are squeezed together on one of the couches, swaying and dancing to the Celsius song that's playing when Connor stands up to get everyone's attention.

He claps his hands twice and calls out, "Yo!" I stifle a giggle and take a sip of my pop. Who says, *Yo?* I'm kind of embarrassed for him. Connor continues, "Thanks for coming to the party of the year, guys!" The boys all start whooping and clapping. Connor is grinning from ear to ear. He is loving it. "Let's finish this pizza," he turns to Hunter, who immediately goes to the table and puts two pieces into his mouth, "and then we'll move the festivities outside to have a fire!"

Everyone cheers, and I swear Connor looks over at me. My heart skips a beat again. Is he going to kiss me under the stars? I swoon at the idea.

8:09 P.M.
AROUND THE FIRE

It took a little while for Connor's dad to get the fire started, but it's roaring now. We're all gathered around, sitting in chairs or on blankets on the ground. Cher, Ruby, and I are sitting together on a blanket right in front of the fire.

"Connoooor," Audrey whines from her chair across from us. "Will you roast my marshmallow for me? You did it so perfectly the last time I was here." The last time she was here? When was that? Ruby and Cher are also watching Audrey act like a helpless nitwit. Ruby's nose is wrinkled, and Cher is watching intently, her lips slightly pursed.

Ruby leans over Cher, so we can both hear her imitate Audrey: "Connoooor, can you help me?" I laugh, but I still feel uneasy. Connor told me they didn't hang out. He walks over to Audrey, grabs the roasting stick from her, and jabs it into the fire.

Audrey looks over at us. She smirks and then leans over to whisper something in Zoe's ear. They both burst into giggles and look in our direction again. "Thanks, Connor. You're the best," she says in a voice I'm sure she thinks sounds sweet, but to me sounds like a dying bird.

My chest tightens, and I feel a rush of heat course through my veins. "Audrey is literally the worst," I complain. I'm careful to be only loud enough for Ruby and Cher to hear me. I can't tell if I'm annoyed at Audrey for being so obnoxious or jealous that she's been here before. Probably both.

Ruby rolls her eyes and hands me a marshmallow in response. Cher doesn't say anything, popping her own marshmallow into her mouth.

8:26 P.M.

"I'm thirsty," I announce from our spot on the blanket. "Come with me to get another drink."

Ruby hops up. "I could go for another orange pop. I never drink pop. My mom says it makes me crazy, but I don't think that's true." Ruby is talking really, really fast.

Cher pulls Ruby by her arm back down onto the blanket. "You don't need any more pop. Plus, Emma's not actually thirsty.

Look who's over there." She nods at the table that now hosts the pop and snacks, where Connor happens to be standing.

"Ooooh, go get him, tiger," Ruby says with a wink, "but also bring me back an orange pop." She gives me a thumbs-up.

"One of you has to come with me." I can't go alone. I'm nervous just being in Connor's house. I can't waltz up to him and start talking. What would I even say?

"No," Cher says. "I have to keep Ruby away from the pop."

Ruby mumbles something about "pop" and "crazy" under her breath.

I hesitate, hovering above my friends. I look over at Connor and then back to Cher and Ruby. Once again, some sort of drum practice is taking place in my chest. Can I actually do this?

"Go," Cher says. "You can do it."

Okay, I guess I can.

I slowly walk over to the snack table and grab a cup. "Hey," I say to Connor. Was that okay? Is my voice as high-pitched as it sounded in my brain? Why can't I be normal? I'm such a loser. I glance over my shoulder at Cher and Ruby. They're staring. Ruby waves and shakes her empty pop can at me.

"Hey," Connor says with a smile. "Just the girl I was hoping to talk to."

"Really?" He wants to talk to me? About what?

"Of course." He puts his plate down on the snack table and takes a step closer to me. "Are you having fun?"

"Totally." *Oh my God, Emma. Don't sound like such a loser.* I shift my weight to one side and pop my hip. *Be cool. Be cute.* "It's a great party. The fire is... um... great." *Great, you're a loser.* I'm out of words. I don't really know what else to say. And for some reason, I'm afraid to look up at him. I sneak a glance, and he smiles again. All his features are dark, but the light from the fire moves across his face every couple of seconds.

"Hey," he starts.

"Hey," I respond.

He laughs. "You're goofy." He takes another step closer. He's so close I can smell him—a mixture of campfire and cologne.

Is this it? It's not, though, because Audrey comes bursting over.

"Connoooor!" she wails. "Come back over by the fire and take a selfie with me." Audrey totally ignores my existence, trying to insert herself between us. I take a step back.

"Audrey—" he starts to say, but she cuts him off.

"No excuses. Let's go!" She grabs his hand and pulls him back over to the fire.

I stand there with my mouth hanging slightly open.

As he's being dragged away, he sort of shrugs his shoulders. "Sorry," he calls back to me.

I give a half-hearted wave in response. Audrey ruins everything.

8:38 P.M.

I throw myself onto the blanket with Ruby and Cher. "Ugggghhh! I seriously hate Audrey. She is. The. Worst!" I don't hold back. Luckily, the sounds of the party drown out my voice.

"What happened?" Ruby asks. "And where is my pop?"

"No more pop, Ruby!" Cher scolds her. She turns back to me. "What happened?"

I explain how Connor and I were chatting, how he was so close I could smell him, and then how Audrey ruined everything. "It was perfect, right up until the end," I whine.

Cher nods and then stares at the fire quietly. Ruby starts bashing Audrey, and I happily join in.

"She should really get some bangs to cover her fivehead." Ruby stops abruptly. "Okay, Emma, don't freak. Be cool."

"What? Why? What are you talking about?" My heart starts racing again. Cher whips her head back toward us. She pushes a piece of hair behind her ear.

I look over my shoulder. Connor is walking over to us.

8:51 P.M.

"Ladies, hello," Connor says, towering over us.

"Gentleman, hello," Ruby responds, tipping an imaginary hat at him.

"Hi, Connor," Cher says loudly and confidently. Sometimes I wish I was more like her. She never seems nervous around boys. I'm nervous around boys I don't even have a crush on.

"Hey," I say meekly. I'm not quirky like Ruby or confident like Cher. Why would Connor like me anyway? I rub at a spot of dirt on my Converse.

"Emma, can I talk to you for a minute?"

I pick my head up, surprised. Ruby has a satisfied smirk on her face, and Cher has a casual, almost bored look on hers. Ruby pokes me. I guess I haven't said anything yet. "Yeah," I say a little too loudly. I stand up and follow him back toward the snack table.

"Bring me a pop!" Ruby shouts after us.

"Sorry about Audrey earlier," he says, grabbing a couple of chips and putting them in his mouth.

For real this time, Emma. Be cool. I roll my eyes and force out a small laugh. "It wasn't a big deal."

"I think it was," he says, his tone serious. I realize now that I haven't been looking at him but rather out at the rest of the party. My eyes go to his face, again covered in shadows, and my heart skips. I swallow hard.

Connor looks around and grabs my hand. He pulls me toward the side of the house. No one else is around. The sounds of the party are muffled. My heart is beating so hard and so fast, I think it might run away. Once again, Connor is so close I can smell him. I take a deep breath, but I'm afraid to look at him again. I shift my focus upward on his ear. It's a nice ear.

He clears his throat and says, "Can I kiss you?"

I am at a loss for words. Literally. I feel like I'm frozen to the ground. I nod.

"Was that a yes? It's dark and kind of hard to see you." There's a catch in his voice. Is he nervous, too?

"Yes," I say with as much confidence as I can muster.

He leans down and softly places his mouth on mine. It feels like everything around us has stopped. All I can feel are Connor's lips on mine.

I think I may have died and gone to heaven.

9:04 P.M.

"You guys!" I practically scream, walking back to Ruby and Cher. I'm trying to stay composed in case Connor is watching. I turn to check, and his back is to me. I wave my arms and hop into the air like a loon to get their attention. One of Connor's baseball friends gives me a strange look, so I put my arms down and continue walking as fast as I can without full-on sprinting.

"You didn't bring me my pop," Ruby complains when I sit down on the blanket.

"Unimportant," I say, waving her off. "Guess what happened over there?"

"Connor asked to be your boyfriend?" Cher guessed.

"Better," I tell them. I feel like I'm floating; I'm so happy.

"Connor asked you to marry him?" Ruby exclaims.

"No." I push her over. She pops back up immediately, brushing off her shoulder. "He kissed me!" We all start squealing and wiggling around on the blanket.

"So, when do you think he'll ask you to be his girlfriend?" Ruby asks once we settle down.

I still have butterflies in my stomach, and I feel slightly lightheaded. "I don't know. Do you think he's going to ask later? He told me to let him know when I have to leave."

"Maybe," Cher says slowly, "but I've also heard that Connor doesn't really like to have a girlfriend."

"What does that even mean?" Ruby shouts, throwing her hands up in the air. She glares at Connor's back.

"Okay, settle down, Ruby." I put my hand on her arm, and she turns back to Cher and me. "Who told you that, Cher?"

"I don't remember," she says, looking down at her phone.

My heart sinks. How can I go from tingling with excitement to being disappointed so fast? If he kissed me, doesn't that mean he likes me? Why wouldn't he want to be my boyfriend if he likes me? I watch the flames dance in the fire, quietly contemplating all of this.

"Hmmmm..." Ruby stands up to get a better view of Connor. "Well, he does seem happy. And asking to kiss you was a gentleman move. Maybe he will ask to be your boyfriend before we leave. But, Emma, do not kiss him again if he doesn't." She says all of this at full volume.

"Ruby!" I hiss. "Sit down. Someone might hear you." I pull her down by her arm. My cheeks are warm. Thank God it's dark.

"Okay. We can return to this conversation later," Ruby says, adjusting herself on the blanket.

"How was the kiss?" Cher asks, putting her phone down.

Ruby leans forward. "Did he use tongue?"

"No, there was no tongue. It was nice." My heart skips thinking about it. In a whisper, I add, "He has very soft lips."

"Do you want to do it again?" Ruby asks slyly.

"Yes." I can't help but smile, and I put my hands over my face to hide it. We all burst into giggles.

9:28 P.M.

"Emma, we should probably go wait for your mom," Ruby says.

"Yeah, you're right." I sigh and reluctantly drag myself up. We've been having so much fun dissecting my kiss with Connor, and every time I see him, I feel a flutter in my chest. Ruby starts walking toward the gate to head straight to the front. "Wait," I call. "I have to tell Connor I'm leaving." I whisper, "Come with me."

"I'm going to run to the bathroom while you do that, Emma," Cher says.

"We can go with you in a second, Cher," Ruby says. "Don't you want to say bye?"

"No, go ahead. I'll meet you out front." She turns to head inside, moving quickly.

We walk over to Connor, who is sitting in a chair in front of the fire. He's laughing with Hunter when Ruby taps him on the shoulder.

"Hey," he says, turning to look at us.

"Hey," I say casually, "we have to go. My mom's picking us up."

"Aw, man, okay. Thanks for coming." He stands up and gives Ruby a quick hug first. Then he opens his arms to me. I walk into them, and he squeezes me tightly. As he does, he says quietly, "I'll text you tomorrow. Maybe we can hang out?" I nod into his shoulder. Then he kisses me on the cheek. In front of everyone. The boys all start "Oohing" and make other whooping noises.

And even though I know my cheeks are as red as a fire hydrant, I smile.

Best. Night. Ever.

9:31 P.M.

"No Cher?" Mom asks when we get in the car.

"She's coming." I hop in the front seat.

"She went to the bathroom," Ruby adds from behind me.

"There she is." Cher's walking to the car. She glances back over her shoulder.

"Took you long enough," Ruby says. "Were you pooping?" She pokes Cher in the arm playfully.

"Ew, Ruby, don't be gross," Cher says, buckling her seat belt. "I was on the phone with my mom."

"How is your mom, Cher?" Mom asks as she shifts the car into drive. "I haven't seen her in ages."

"She's fine. She has a new boyfriend," Cher says.

"She does?" Ruby exclaims. "Why didn't you tell us? What's his name? What does he look like? What's his job?"

"Who cares. He'll be gone soon enough," Cher snaps. She turns to stare out the window, looking sullen. Mom subtly shakes her head, which I take to mean, "Let's drop it." We ride home in silence.

Even in the silence, I can't stop smiling. *Connor kissed me! Twice!*

10:13 P.M.
BEDROOM

Ruby and I are on the floor, making a nest of blankets and once again discussing my kiss with Connor.

"What do you think the cheek-kiss meant, though?" I ask.

"I don't know, but I think it's a good sign that he did it in front of everyone," Ruby says knowingly.

I plop down on the blankets and sigh. "His lips are so soft," I say dreamily.

"Oh my God. Can you guys shut up about it already?" Cher suddenly bursts out. "You didn't even make out!" Ruby and I stare at her, shocked. Now her cheeks are red. "I'm going to bed. If you guys want to keep blabbering on about Emma's 'kiss,'"—she uses air quotes on the word "kiss"—"can you go downstairs and do it?" Then she digs in her bag to find her toothbrush and storms out of my bedroom.

11:33 P.M.
BED

Ruby and I decided to go to bed with Cher. Something is definitely up with her. We followed her into the bathroom, brushed our teeth, and went to bed without saying anything else.

"Night, guys," I quietly said as I crawled into bed.

"Goodnight, my beautiful friends," Ruby mumbled next to me, already half asleep.

"Night," Cher said dully from the nest of blankets.

But of course, here I am an hour later, and I can't fall asleep. Everything from tonight keeps running through my mind—Connor, Audrey, Connor, Cher, Connor. (Okay, mostly Connor.)

Will he text me tomorrow? Does he want to be my boyfriend? Do I let him kiss me again, even if he's not my boyfriend?

Is it bad that I want to?

CHAPTER 19

Who cares what he calls it!

SUNDAY, MAY 2ND
11:30 A.M.
BEDROOM

Mom knocks on the door and peeks her head around the corner. "Can I come in?" I nod from my spot on my bed. "The girls left pretty quickly this morning," she notes.

I nod again. "Ruby was going to her grandma's. Cher was being... weird."

"Is something going on with her?" Mom walks over and sits on the bed with me. I shrug. I don't even know what's going on with Cher. "Be patient with her. She'll talk to you when she's ready."

I shrug again. "Okay."

"Soooo?" she says, shaking my knee.

"Soooo, what?" I glance down at my phone. No text from Connor yet. I put it face down on my bed.

"Oh, come on. You were cheesing so hard when you got into the car last night."

"I don't know what you're talking about." I grab my phone again and scroll through the pictures we took yesterday, examining my face.

Mom grabs the phone from my hand. "Come on," she whines. "Give me something. Are you already too cool to tell your mom your secrets?" I raise my eyebrows, but I don't say anything. She sighs. "I guess you are. I knew this day would come eventually, but I didn't know it would come so fast." She pretends to cry into her hands. I lean over and put my arm around her, pretending to console her. She lifts her head. "Will you give me one, teensy, tiny detail?"

"Maybe." I am *not* discussing the kiss with my mom. No way. Too embarrassing.

"Did you have a good night?" is all she asks.

"Yes." I can't help it. I'm smiling again.

She leans over and kisses my head. "Remember what I said, sweetie. Okay?"

"Yes, Mom, I know." I roll my eyes, but I'm also still smiling as she gets up.

"*Mom!*" Marie shouts from downstairs.

"Duty calls," Mom says. As she walks out the door, she shouts back, "Coming!"

I lean back onto my pillows. I can't believe Mom was so almost-cool there. I'm about to reach for my laptop when my phone dings.

I lunge for it. My stomach does a flip-flop when I see the name on the screen. It's Connor.

12:09 P.M.
I am going to Connor's house. Today. At 2:00. Ahhhh!

1:15 P.M.

I text Ruby and Cher to tell them about my looming adventure. I'm already so nervous. My hands are shaking as I type the message. I get about ten responses from Ruby, all right in a row.

Ruby: You have to tell us EVERYTHING. IMMEDIATELY!

When will you be home?

Text me in the car on your way home.

No. Scratch that. Call me.

Can I come over?

Oh shoot, I can't. I'm supposed to watch a movie with my mom tonight. *Eye-roll emoji*

Good luck! Remember YOU ARE AWESOME!

Nothing from Cher, though...

1:56 P.M.
EN ROUTE

I might die before we make it to Connor's. My heart is thumping, my hands are sweating, and I have to keep swallowing a lump in my throat.

Mom is trying to talk to me, but I don't even know what she's saying.

"Mom, I can't talk right now," I squeak out.

Mom sighs. "Okay, Em. I'll pick you up at four-thirty. Text me if you want to come home earlier."

Oh my God. Oh my God. Oh my God! We're at Connor's house. Mom is pulling in the driveway. I text Connor that I'm here.

"Did you hear me, Emma?"

"What? Yes." No, I didn't. She knows this.

"If you want to come home but don't want to say that, send me a text that's just 'K.' I'll know what you mean." Her eyes are wide, and she's not blinking. I can't deal with this right now.

"Okay, Mom, got it. 'K.'" I open the car door and hop out.

Connor is waiting for me with his perfect face, beautiful eyes, and soft lips. I swoon, and I think my legs might give out, but I make it to the door without collapsing.

Be cool, Emma!

2:41 P.M.
CONNOR'S BASEMENT

I can't believe I'm at Connor's house. Hanging out in his basement. With him.

After he greeted me at the door, we said hi to his parents and then came downstairs to watch a movie. This is so cool. Mom and Dad would never let me hang out with a boy alone like this—let's face it, Dad wasn't crazy about me hanging out with a boy at all.

"Who's Connor? Why are you going there?" he grumbled.

"We're partners in science. Remember?"

He kept grumbling, but Mom shuffled me out the door. When did she start being so normal?

I pull myself back to the present moment. Sitting next to Connor. I still have butterflies in my stomach. Will I ever stop being nervous? Luckily, Connor is doing most of the talking. He put on a movie I've never seen before—it's about some baseball team or something. Not that we're really watching it anyway. Connor is talking through most of it—about his baseball team, his brother's football team, where he's going to go to college to play baseball, his record in baseball. I would normally think this is very boring, but I'm with *Connor*—the boy I've had a crush on forever, the boy I thought didn't know I existed.

We're sitting on the couch, facing each other more than the TV. I can *feel* him close to me. I can smell him, too. From now on, I will always equate the scent of *Axe Black Chill* (I checked when I went to the bathroom) with Connor. He starts to quiet down, turning toward the TV.

"This is my favorite part," he says, putting his hand next to mine. It's so close our pinky fingers are almost touching. Does he want me to hold his hand? Do I grab it? No. Maybe I should... I move my pinky finger a millimeter closer so it barely touches his. He turns and smiles, and then he grabs my hand.

I feel a jolt of energy go through my body when he touches me. I try to memorize how it feels to have my hand in his. His hands are a little hard—probably from baseball—and warm. As I examine his hand, I notice his fingernails, and my cheeks warm.

They're long. They aren't witch's fingernails, but they're longer than, like, my dad's nails, and it weirds me out. I push it out of my brain because this is *Connor*, who is basically perfect. I decide that as long as I don't look at them, it won't be a problem.

Connor shifts back toward me again. I glance up at the movie and then to my left. Connor is staring back at me. My heart starts thumping in my chest. Something is about to happen. I can feel it. I don't know what to do. I examine our intertwined hands again and then pretend to be very interested in the grayish-blue carpet of the basement.

"Emma," he says. I force my gaze up to meet his. It's like he's pretty—those eyes, those lips, honestly who cares about his fingernails? Look at his face! "Do you want to French kiss?"

My stomach twists. That's... weird. Who says French kiss? For some reason, it really bothers me. Once again, I push it out of my mind. *Who cares what he calls it? He wants to make out with you!* I give a slight nod, biting my lip.

"Have you ever French kissed someone before?"

Stop saying French kiss! I want to shout, but instead, I shake my head. "Sorry."

He chuckles and gets up from the couch. "Don't be sorry. I can teach you. Here, stand up." He pulls me up to face him. "Okay, it's like when I kissed you last night, except I'm going to put my tongue in your mouth."

"I mean, I know how it works." I'm not a complete idiot.

"Let's do it then," he says with a lopsided smile. My heart pounds even harder if that's possible. He takes a step closer and leans in...

7:17 P.M.

HOME

My mind is a whirlwind of emotions.

I ignore the texts from Ruby for a while (still no word from Cher), but she's been sending one every ten minutes for the past hour. Finally, I can't take it anymore.

Me: I'll tell you about it tomorrow.

Ruby: Is everything okay?

Me: Yes. Tomorrow!

Then I turn my phone off, so I can think.

7:38 P.M.

It was good. I think.

7:40 P.M.

But weird. It was weird.

CHAPTER 20

It just kind of sat there in my mouth.

MONDAY, MAY 3RD
8:07 A.M.
OUTSIDE SCHOOL

"It just kind of sat in my mouth," I tell them.

"No, that's not right, Emma," Cher says knowingly.

"It was weird. And he kept calling it 'French kissing.'"

"Ew," Ruby gasps.

"I know, right?" It makes me feel slightly better that they also think this is not normal.

"Did you move your tongue?" Cher asks.

"Well, no. He knew I'd never done it before. I was following his lead."

Cher nods slowly.

"What happened next?" Ruby demands. "Every. Detail. Remember? You made me wait more than twelve hours to hear the tea."

"Not much happened after that," I tell them. "We sat back down on the couch and finished watching the movie. We held hands. He kissed me again before I left—"

"With or without tongue?" Cher questioned.

"Without. Then I went home. He texted me right when I got home and said, 'It was fun hanging out today,' with a winky face. I said, 'Definitely,' with a smiley face. Then I turned my phone off."

"You don't seem very excited, Emma," Ruby says.

"Yeah, I don't know..."

It wasn't what I was expecting. I thought the first time I made out with a boy would be romantic and wonderful, but this was... not. It makes me feel weird and twisty inside.

"Do you want to hang out with him again?" Cher asks.

"No, more importantly: Are you going to kiss him again?" Ruby interjects.

"I don't know. What if he feels this way too?"

"What way?" Ruby asks.

"Like... I don't know... like it was weird..."

"I doubt it. Boys don't think about these things as much as girls," Cher says, once again sharing her wisdom. I nod.

"Plus, he's still your partner in science," Ruby adds. "The rollercoasters aren't due for another week."

My stomach drops when I realize she's right.

9:24 A.M.
SCIENCE

Connor's not in school today. I wonder why. He seemed fine yesterday.

Am I a bad kisser? Was I supposed to do more? I feel queasy every time I think about it. I'm kind of glad he's not in school. This way I can try to figure out how I'm feeling without being distracted by his beautiful face.

9:57 A.M.

I notice Hunter biting his nails. Why can't Connor bite his nails so they're a normal length?

Why do his nails bother me so much?

9:59 A.M.

But why are they like that? I feel like you shouldn't see any white bits on boys' nails.

LUNCH

"What are your thoughts on boys' nails?" I ask.

"Their nails? Like their fingernails?" Ruby shows me her hand. "Or their toenails?" She starts to pick up her foot, but Cher puts her arm out to stop Ruby.

"Gross. Their fingernails," I say.

"Why?" Cher asks.

"Just curious." I don't really want to share the thing about Connor's nails. I'm not sure why. "Shouldn't they be short?"

Ruby thinks for a second, munching on some Cheetos. Cher takes a sip of her pop and then says, "Yeah, I think they should probably be short, I guess. I've never really thought about it."

"But if they wanted to keep them long, they should be able to," Ruby counters.

Cher rolls her eyes. "What, are you and your future boyfriend going to give each other manicures, Ruby?"

"Actually, that sounds like fun." Ruby looks at me and shrugs. "Doesn't it?"

I laugh and then change the subject to something else.

8:17 P.M.
BEDROOM

I looked up some kissing techniques in case I'm a bad kisser. I read an article called *Becoming a Sex Goddess: Making Out 101.* Here's what I've discovered:

- *Make eye contact before you start.* This may be a problem. I could barely look at Connor yesterday.

- *Move slowly to avoid headbutting or teeth crashing.* Teeth crashing? That happens?

- *You should add in the tongue slowly.* Does this mean not putting it in his mouth right away? Or moving it around slowly once it's inside his mouth?

- *Don't stab his tongue with yours. No one wants to kiss a lizard.* Ew. Definitely not.

- *Put your hands on his face. Stroke his hair. Don't let your arms dangle by your side.* I don't even know what I did with my arms.

- *Don't have bad breath.* Okay, duh. That one I knew.

- *If it's heating up, let out a quiet groan to let him know you like it.* What does heating up mean? And groan? I don't think so.

- *Change things up. Vary the pressure you use.* With my lips or my tongue?

- *Nibble his bottom lip.* How hard? For how long?

- *Whisper something in his ear, such as, "You're so sexy."* Nope.

- *Confidence is key.* Ha! You're funny, sex goddess.

- *Go with the flow.* That's what I tried to do!

Oh, boy. I have a lot of learning to do.

8:30 P.M.
What is wrong with me? I just tried to make out with my hand. There are a lot of kissing tutorials on the internet.
I feel gross.

8:38 P.M.
But, I mean, it has to be helpful, right? I sort of feel like I'm getting the hang of slowly introducing my tongue.

8:41 P.M.
My bedroom door bursts open. "What are you doing?" Marie asks slowly, standing in the doorway.

I shoot up out of my chair so fast I knock it over. "Oh my God! Ever heard of knocking? What are you doing in here?"

"What are *you* doing?" she asks again, with a smirk on her face. "Were you kissing your *hand*?" I don't say anything. I feel the heat creep up into my face. "You were. Weren't you?" Her eyes go wide, and she breaks into a huge smile.

"I swear to God, Marie, if you don't get out of here right now—"

"What?" she sneers. "I'll tell Mom you were practicing to kiss Connor again." She pops her knee and starts bouncing, proud that she's such a good eavesdropper.

"You really need to mind your own business and get out of my room." I'm trying not to yell because Mom will come up here, and I really don't want to exchange kissing techniques with her. Ew! Now I'm picturing her and Dad making out. Ahhhh. Make it stop! I rub my eyes to get rid of the disgusting picture in my head.

"Why are you here?" I demand.

She shrugs. "No reason, really. I'm bored."

This makes me so mad; I swear I see red for a second. *"Get out!"* I say through clenched teeth. She stares back at me, blinking twice. I take a step toward her, and she turns and runs down the hallway into her room. She slams the door. I slam mine in response.

Dad shouts from the living room, "Girls! Cut it out!"

8:44 P.M.
I can't believe my sister caught me kissing my hand.

8:45 P.M.
I can't believe I was kissing my hand.

CHAPTER 21

Have you ever practiced kissing?

TUESDAY, MAY 4TH
8:17 A.M.

As I'm closing my locker, someone taps me on the shoulder. I spin around, expecting Ruby, but it's Connor. At that moment, I forget his fingernails, the floppy tongue, and all the thoughts I've had since Sunday. Connor is standing in front of me. The cutest boy in our grade is standing in front of me. And he kissed me!

"Hey, cutie," he says.

I know I'm blushing, but it's a good kind of blushing. I actually enjoy the warmth spreading across my cheeks and in my chest.

"Hey," I say back. Why can't I think of any clever greetings? I make a mental note to brainstorm witty ways to say "Hey," later.

"Did you miss me yesterday?"

I giggle and blush even harder. "Yeah. Where were you?"

"Avoiding the math quiz." He smirks. "Sorry to bail on you in science."

"That's okay. I got more work done without you there to distract me," I tease him. He laughs. Hey, maybe I am getting better at this. And maybe I was wrong about the kissing. I don't know what I'm doing. I just need to practice more. With him, though. Not my hand. I blush again, thinking about my practice yesterday.

"Where are your sidekicks?" Connor asks.

"That's a good question." I glance down the hall. "They mumbled something about science when we came in, but I wasn't really listening."

"Shall we?" He gestures toward Ms. Stein's classroom. I nod and giggle, stepping into stride with him. I smile to myself. How did this happen to me?

3:04 P.M.
WALKING HOME

"Have you ever *practiced* kissing?" I ask Ruby. Marie went home with one of her little friends after school, so I don't need to worry about her hearing this conversation.

"What do you mean?" Ruby stops walking. "Actually, it doesn't matter what you mean. Either way, my answer is no." She wiggles her eyebrows at me. "Have you?"

I groan, but not in the sex goddess way I also practiced. Although they sound basically the same. I start walking again, so I don't have to look at her. "Are you going to make fun of me if I say yes?"

"Definitely," she says, but she hip-bumps me at the same time. Even though she might think it's silly, Ruby wouldn't actually make fun of me, at least not in a way that would make me feel bad about myself. I was afraid if I told Cher, she would make me feel like a baby who doesn't know anything about kissing. Which I don't, but I don't want to feel any more stupid than I already do on the subject.

I explain what happened last night—the research, the practice, Marie barging in. Ruby bursts into laughter.

"Marie saw you?" she says between fits of laughter. I give her the evil eye. "Girl, don't stank eye me. You know I can do it better than anyone else." We stop again, and she raises her eyebrows, narrows her eyes, and purses her lips. She looks me up and down before she turns her head the other way with an eye-roll that puts even Cher's to shame.

"Whoa!" I put my hands up in surrender.

"I know." She smiles, pleased with herself, and starts walking again. "Anyway, continue. Your sister saw you making out with your hand..." Ruby loops her arm through mine as we continue walking down the street.

By the time I finish explaining it to her and promise to show her how to do it at our next sleepover, we're in front of Ruby's house. We stop at the driveway, and I see that Georgia's black SUV isn't there yet. "To be honest, Em," Ruby says, "I don't think there's anything wrong with it. In fact," she holds up a finger to make a point, "I think it's smart!"

"Really?" I ask skeptically. "It's not... weird? Or creepy?"

"Maybe a little. But..." She narrows her eyes and lowers her voice like she's telling a secret. "It's smart. You're practicing and getting better, so by the time you kiss Connor again, you'll be a sex goddess."

I push her away. "Ruby! I don't want to be a sex goddess."

She shrugs. "I do. I'm going to go home and make out with my hand all day." She makes a fist with her hand and gives it a big, wet kiss. Then she looks directly at me and flicks her tongue at her hand like a lizard.

We burst into one of those fits of laughter where you can't breathe. I'm bent in half with a pain in my stomach, and Ruby's laughing so hard she has tears streaking her face, but neither of us can stop.

Once we've finally calmed down, Ruby says, "Okay, I need to go in and eat something. All that practice made me hungry. Text me later, Em." She starts to make her way to the side door, but she turns when I call her name.

"Love you, weirdo."

"Back atcha." She waves and runs the rest of the way to the door.

FRIDAY, MAY 7TH
LUNCH

The three of us are sitting at our lunch table, discussing kissing techniques when I get a tap on my shoulder. It's Audrey and Zoe.

"Emma," Audrey scoffs, standing above me, "I want you to know you can *have* Connor. I don't even care about him anymore." She smirks over her shoulder at Zoe, who giggles and nods. "I mean, been there, done that." She flips her hair over her shoulder and turns to walk away. Before she does, though, she says, "Cher, text me later." Then she links her arm through Zoe's, and they walk back to their lunch table.

"Um, what just happened?" Ruby asks, looking from Cher to me and back again.

"Cher? Did you tell Audrey about Connor and me?" I feel stiff like I can't move any part of my body. Cher glances up at me and then over to where Audrey and Zoe are sitting.

"I didn't know it was a secret," she says without emotion. She stares blankly back at me.

Ruby's eyes are wide in disbelief. For once, she's at a loss for words.

"I mean... I guess it's not," I say quietly. My lunch is slowly churning in my stomach. Even if it wasn't a secret,

I don't think Audrey, who is basically my sworn enemy, needs to know who I've been kissing. What Cher did was not okay.

Cher shrugs and goes back to her lunch.

"But…" I hesitate. I don't want to start a fight. But I'm mad. And confused. "Why would you tell Audrey?"

Cher lifts her gaze to mine. Her eyebrows are slightly raised, and her lips are pursed. She sighs and rolls her eyes. "She asked me. She's seen the two of you walking in the hallway together. And obviously, the rollercoaster partner thing. So I told her." Cher continues staring at me, not breaking eye contact. It feels like a dare to keep going.

"Oh," is all I say. I pick at my sandwich. Why is Cher even talking to Audrey? And when is she talking to Audrey? I take a deep breath. "But—"

Cher cuts me off. "You really need to grow up, Emma." She stands up suddenly. "I have to pee," she mumbles, walking toward the front of the lunchroom.

Ruby and I look at each other, but neither of us says anything. Ruby slowly shakes her head before turning back to her lunch. I feel a prickle behind my eyes and stare down at the table, not hungry. The sounds of other people's conversations, chairs scraping, and garbage plunking become white noise, and in my chest, I feel a spark burst into flame.

2:07 P.M.
SOCIAL STUDIES

What the hell is going on with Cher? She's been acting weird for over a week now. Is she jealous of Connor and me? Why can't she be happy for me? Isn't that what friends are supposed to do? She knows how much I like Connor and how long I've liked him. Which is, like, forever.

2:09 P.M.

And, "Text me later, Cher"? What was that about? Since when does Cher even have Audrey's number? Something smells fishy.

2:39 P.M.

HOMEROOM

"Okay, friends, don't forget that our field trip is a week from today," Ms. Stein announces. There are a couple of groans from the class, including a loud one from Alejandra behind me.

"I can't believe we're being forced to do this," she complains.

I nod in agreement but don't turn around. I'm still too upset to even make fun of this field trip.

"I know. I know," Ms. Stein concedes. "It's important, though." She's standing at the front of the room, waving her arms around for emphasis. Today she has on a long, blue and green skirt with some sort of feathery pattern. It's kind of ugly, but it looks like it would be comfortable. "Look on the bright side. We're going out for lunch afterward." Ms. Stein runs her hand through her somewhat frizzy, wavy hair. Even with the frizz, I wish my hair was that cool and effortless. A few people cheer in response to the announcement about lunch. Hunter actually gets out of his seat to go high-five Connor. Everyone laughs, including Ms. Stein.

I look over at Connor, and he smiles back at me with his perfectly straight teeth and perfectly plump lips. I can't wait to kiss them again. *Wow, stop it, Emma.* Maybe I *am* a sex goddess. My cheeks warm. I turn back toward Ms. Stein, and Cher catches my attention.

She's staring at Connor. With gooey eyes. The way *I* stare at Connor. I blink and shake my head. I must be imagining it. She just happened to be looking that way. But when I open my eyes again, she's still staring, and now she has her pen in her mouth.

I hope it explodes, and she gets blue ink all over her face.

3:02 P.M.

I'm so pissed that I don't even wait for Ruby to start walking. All I want to do is get home and snuggle my cat. I'm blinking back the prickling behind my eyes when I hear someone—a boy—call my name.

I take a deep breath and turn around. Connor's jogging to catch up to me.

"Hey! Geez, you really ran out of there today." He throws his arm across my shoulders. OhmyGodOhmyGodOhmyGod. This is amazing. Suck it, Audrey. And Cher.

"Yeah." I'm not going to give him the details.

And he doesn't ask, which is a relief. "Anyways, I wanted to talk to you," he says. My heart immediately starts racing. His dark hair is falling into his eyes a little bit. He uses the arm not around my shoulders to push it back. He is *so* cool. He stops walking. "Actually, can we stop? I live in the opposite direction, so my walk is going to get longer and longer if we keep going your way." He laughs. I laugh. We are so cute. "So, I was thinking. We should probably hang out and work on our rollercoaster project..."

"Well, there's not much we can do without the actual rollercoaster."

He smiles down at me, and my heart melts into a puddle. "True. Maybe we should make out instead?"

My gaze goes to my feet. I know my cheeks are flaming. I force myself to look up at him again, and I can't help it. I'm smiling like a little kid in a candy shop. I nod.

"Awesome," he says with a lopsided smile. He adjusts the shoulder of his backpack and glances to his right. "How about a quick one right now?"

Now? What if someone sees? A little piece of me hopes someone does.

"Okay."

He spins me so that I'm fully facing him, and I let out a giggle. He leans down. I put my face up toward his, ready to practice some of the maneuvers I've been trying. *Watch the teeth! Watch the teeth!*

3:07 P.M.

"Oh my God!" Ruby's bellow breaks the bliss, and I tear myself away from Connor's wonderful, minty, delicious, slightly slobbery mouth. I try to discreetly wipe my own mouth on my sleeve.

"Oh my *God!*" she shouts again, walking up to us, pointing her finger up and down. "What is going on here?" She winks. My face feels like it is going to burst into flames at any second. Connor has a goofy, dazed look on his face like a puppy caught chewing a shoe. I bust out laughing hard, clutching my stomach with laughter.

Connor looks down at me, stunned for a second, and then he lets out a nervous laugh. "I'll text you later, Emma," he says, crouching down to my level. I'm still laughing and holding my stomach.

I take a deep breath and stand up. "Yeah, for sure." He leans in to kiss me again, I think, but Ruby loudly clears her throat.

"Okay, then. Bye, ladies." He turns and jogs down the street.

"Oh my God!" Ruby squeals.

I make sure Connor's out of earshot before I also squeal, "I know!"

We're hopping up and down, squealing in delight, when my mom pulls up next to us. "Need a ride?"

Marie eyes us suspiciously from the front seat. "What are you doing?"

"Nothing," Ruby and I say in unison. We look at each other and once again burst into giggles.

CHAPTER 22

It's good to be unplugged for a while.

3:09 P.M.
IN THE CAR

"We're going to go to Grandma's for the weekend," Mom announces from the front seat.

"Yay!" Marie shouts next to her. Mom usually picks her up on Fridays.

I groan inwardly. "All weekend?" Mom will occasionally spring last-minute trips like this on us, and it drives me crazy. What if I had plans? (I don't, but she doesn't know that.) I love my grandma and all, but do I need to spend the entire weekend with her? I don't think so. Plus, we were there for her birthday like a month ago.

"Yep," Mom says.

"Can Ruby come?" *Please say yes. Please say yes.* I grab Ruby's hand to seal my silent wish. I don't think I can stand an entire weekend with only Marie for company.

"No. Sorry, girls." I open my mouth to argue. Mom gives me a death stare in the rearview mirror. "Don't start," she snaps. I close my mouth. I lean down in my seat to sulk.

Ruby scooches over and lays her head on my shoulder. She whispers, "Text me as soon as you can. We have so much to discuss."

My heart soars thinking about the kissing, but then almost immediately it drops, and my stomach twists when I remember—Cher.

4:12 P.M.
BACK IN THE CAR

It takes two hours to get to my grandma's house. We've been in the car for three minutes, and I'm already bored. I put my earbuds in and turn on Celsius's new album, *Heating Up*, which I downloaded before we left. Stephen's voice fills my ears as we get onto the highway; thirty seconds in, James, the real star and my total celebrity crush, starts singing. I close my eyes and let his smooth, deep voice wash over me.

6:59 P.M.
GRANDMA'S

My aunt, uncle, and cousin came over for dinner at Grandma's tonight. I stay quiet and try to look very interested in my mashed potatoes.

That is until Mom says my name. My head jerks up, and she's smiling at me like she's got me cornered.

"Huh?" blurts out of my mouth.

"Huh?" Mom mocks me. I roll my eyes as she and Aunt Pam laugh together. I hope I'm never as lame as them. I'll remember this when I'm a mom; kids don't want to be dragged into your conversations. If we're being quiet, it's because we don't want to tell you every detail of our lives.

"Aunt Pam asked if you had any boyfriends," Mom says, "and I said she should ask you herself." There's that smile again.

I turn my attention back to the mashed potatoes on my plate, but I can feel everyone staring at me. "No comment," I say quietly.

Marie pretends to cough but clearly is saying, "Connor." Everyone laughs, but I keep my eyes on my plate as my face gets warmer and warmer.

"Oh, come on, Emma," Aunt Pam says. "Give us the deets!" She looks at my mom, and once again, they giggle together. So lame.

"There are no *deets* to give. He's just a boy I go to school with."

It's Mom's turn now to roll her eyes. "Sure, Emma, you keep saying that…" But thankfully, they change the subject.

9:07 P.M.
IN BED

I said I was tired, so I could escape my family. They don't give up. At least I'm alone now. I text Ruby. She cuts right to the chase.

Ruby: Tell me EVERYTHING about kissing Connor today! It sure didn't look like it just sat in your mouth this time!

Me: OMG RUBY!! It was amazing!! A little… um… wet, I guess? But so perfect. *Sigh* I can't believe it happened. Out on the street! Where anyone could see us!

Ruby: I KNOW! I SAW YOU, REMEMBER?

Me: Hahahahaha, I know! So embarrassing… How did we look?

Ruby: Adorbs. #CutestCouple But also… kind of gross. HA! (but seriously)

Me: STAHP. Ugh. But why hasn't he asked me out yet?

Ruby: Hmm… that's a good Q… speaking of good Qs…

Me: Cher? SERIOUSLY! What is going on with her?? Since when are she and Audrey texting? AND I didn't have time to tell you earlier, but I saw her looking at Connor in class! Like, with googly eyes.

Ruby: What? Are you sure… Maybe you only think you saw that because you were mad about what happened at lunch??

Me: No, Ruby. I know what I saw.

Ruby: Hmmm… I don't know, Em.

Me: Have you talked to her?

Ruby: Nope. You?

Me: Definitely not.

Ruby: Weird.

Me: Very.

I rest my phone on my stomach for a second, thinking. I replay the lunch debacle in my head, and I'm annoyed all over again.

Me: Ughhhhhhh. And Audrey. "Been there, done that"? She and Connor never went out. Did they??

Ruby: I don't think so… but think about you and him, Em.

And it hits me then. He probably did the same thing with Audrey. My stomach is suddenly in knots. He's not going to ask me to be his girlfriend. Is he?

Of course—because it's just my luck—my phone suddenly has no service. My last text (three frowning emojis) won't even go through to Ruby.

SATURDAY, MAY 8TH
9:58 A.M.

Still no service. I tell Mom, and she says. "It's good to be unplugged for a while. In fact," and she holds out her hand," give me your phone. Let's all go phone-free for the rest of the weekend!"

"What? No way." I get up and start to calmly back out of the room with my phone.

"Emma. I'm serious."

"But, Mom, I—"

"No 'buts,' Emma."

I try to run away, but Mom is surprisingly fast. She grabs me from behind and wrestles the phone from my grasp. Then she runs down the hallway, laughing like a maniac.

10:03 A.M.

What am I going to do? What if someone texts me?

10:05 A.M.

What if Connor texts me! What if he thinks I'm ignoring him?

SUNDAY, MAY 9TH
6:17 A.M.

I burst into Mom's room. "Good morning!" I sing. "Let's go. Time to get up. Let's eat breakfast. We've got to get on the road. Don't we? Don't want to get stuck in traffic."

Mom pulls the covers over her face. "Not going to work, Emma," she mumbles. "Go back to sleep. We're not leaving until this afternoon."

I hate everything. I storm out, slamming the door.

2:15 P.M.
IN THE CAR

Finally! I turn my phone on and give it a minute to load up.

Still no service. I slam the phone down onto my seat and bang my head back against the headrest. Next to me, Marie rolls her eyes.

2:32 P.M.

My phone dings. *Yes!*

I have forty-six messages from Ruby, two from Connor, and none from Cher...

CHAPTER 23

And I don't just have feelings. I have thoughts too.

MONDAY, MAY 10TH
9:30 A.M.
SCIENCE

Connor's still out of town with his family, so I'm working alone on our project. When Ruby and I got to school this morning, Cher was standing with Audrey and Zoe. She looked over her shoulder at us but turned right back to Audrey. Ruby was fuming.

"What is her deal?" she practically shouted.

After Cher's silence over the weekend, I'm not surprised, but it still feels like a punch in the gut. "I don't know. She's been acting weird for weeks now." I pause because I'm afraid I might start crying. I swallow the lump in my throat and continue, "I don't even want to talk to her."

So we haven't. All morning. Even at our lockers. I kept my gaze straight into my locker, and she did the same. We didn't say one word to each other, and once she'd grabbed her books, she went straight to class.

I peek back at Cher and Ruby now. They're both working quietly, their bodies slightly turned away from each other. At least the projects are due Wednesday.

LUNCH

Ruby and I are sitting alone at our usual table. Cher is sitting across the lunchroom with Audrey and Zoe. The three of them are huddled together, giggling. Cher looks up, and I catch her eye. She raises an eyebrow at me.

For some reason, this really sets me off. My cheeks warm, and my heart starts racing. I turn to Ruby. "What the *hell* is Cher's problem? What makes her *better* than us? I bet she's been planning this for weeks. Remember after the argumentative projects? She was talking to Audrey in the morning."

Ruby nods slowly. "Yeah... she was..." She pauses for a second. "Why do you think she doesn't want to be friends with us anymore?" Some of my anger melts away because Ruby sounds so sad. I put my arm around her.

"Forget them!" I squeak in my mouse voice. And then my anger is back like a white-hot flash. Forget Cher. If she wants to ditch us that easily, that's fine with me. Obviously, we don't mean that much to her if she can drop us like it's nothing.

3:08 P.M.
WALKING HOME

"I'm sad," Ruby says.

"Me too," I tell her.

"Why?" Marie asks.

We both ignore her.

"I'm mad, too," Ruby says.

"Me too."

"Why?" Marie asks again.

We ignore her again.

9:12 P.M.

BED

I'm lying here in the dark, staring up at the ceiling. So many emotions and thoughts are floating around in my brain that I don't know what to concentrate on.

When I think about Cher, I'm sad and mad and confused and upset and embarrassed and hurt. But when I think about Connor, I can't help but feel happy and giddy. He likes *me*. Not Audrey. Not Cher. Me. But then, inevitably, I end up back in the loop of sad-mad-confused again because of Cher.

9:18 P.M.

And I don't just have feelings. I have thoughts too. Like, why? Why did Cher ditch us? Was it Audrey's idea or Cher's? Did Cher decide to ditch us? Was she ever really our friend, or has she been waiting for a better opportunity this whole time? What do they talk about? Do they talk about me? Do they make fun of me? Does she tell Audrey things we told her in secret?

Oh, God, I hope she doesn't tell Audrey about the time I pooped at her cottage.

9:39 P.M.

Again I wonder if Cher likes Connor. That's got to be it. It's the only explanation for all of this. She started acting weird and distant as soon as Connor commented on my picture. Why couldn't she be honest with me? How long has this been going on?

Why can't I have one good thing happen to me? Connor *finally* likes me, but I'm going to lose one of my best friends because she's jealous that he likes me instead of her? It's infuriating.

My head feels like it's going to explode.

9:55 P.M.

Am I immature? Do I need to grow up, like Cher says? How can I grow up without boobs anyway?

I run my hands down my chest. Still nothing there. I try to push what teensy tiny bits there are together with my fingers. Why won't they grow?

10:01 P.M.

Why does Connor like me? Does he actually like me? Or is this some weird and cruel ploy to embarrass me?

No. He's not a bully. Plus, he kissed me. In public! He's so dreamy... But I'm still not his girlfriend. Did he kiss Audrey too? Did Audrey tell Cher about it?

10:09 P.M.

A tear slides down the side of my face. I didn't even realize I was going to cry. Another one comes out. I'm back at the beginning again. Why doesn't Cher want to be friends with us anymore? I swat at another tear that escapes.

I thought I didn't care that I was fine with Cher ditching us. I was wrong.

10:32 P.M.

Mom always says not to put your energy into people who don't appreciate you. If Cher doesn't appreciate Ruby and me, she doesn't deserve us anyway. So, I'm not going to give her any more of my energy.

I pull Piggy, my stuffed pig, onto my chest and give him a squeeze. Albus saunters in and lets out a loud meow. He hops up on the bed and starts kneading my stomach. "Thanks, handsome boy." I wipe one last tear from my eye.

WEDNESDAY, MAY 12TH
7:35 A.M.
WALKING TO SCHOOL

Ruby comes storming out of her house. "Let's go!" she demands, turning the corner from her driveway onto the sidewalk. I have to run to catch up to her.

"Whoa! Slow down, Ruby! What are you in such a rush for?" I pant.

Ruby doesn't slow down. She stares straight ahead. "We need to get to school. I need to talk to Cher."

Our rollercoasters are due today, which means Ruby and Cher have to present theirs. Together. (It also means Connor and I have to present ours.) At the end of class yesterday, Cher told Ruby she would do all the talking. Before Ruby could argue, the bell rang, and Cher was gone.

"She is *not* going to make me look like an idiot," Ruby says now.

"No one could make *you* look like an idiot, Rubs."

"Exactly." She keeps walking. I take a deep breath and pick up my pace.

LUNCH

Ruby sits down across from me, beaming from ear to ear.

"You did an amazing job, Ruby!"

"I know," she says, flipping her braids over her shoulder. "It felt so good, you know?"

I nod. Ruby totally took control when we watched their rollercoaster. Every time Cher tried to talk, Ruby cut her off, talking more loudly, and once, even standing right in front of her.

At that point, Mrs. Short said, "Okay, Ruby, why don't you let Cher talk." But it didn't matter. She'd already gotten her point across. And for once, Cher was blushing.

My presentation with Connor went off without a hitch. We planned to let him do most of the talking because I hate presenting. After we were done, he gave me a high five and said, "We crushed it." And we totally did.

Ruby and I eat our lunch as usual, talking about the presentations and sharing chips. All of a sudden, Ruby's eyes narrow. Cher is standing at the end of the table, arms crossed, giving Ruby a death stare.

Ruby stands up and puts her hands on her hips. "Do you need something?"

Cher rolls her eyes and goes to sit with her new BFFs, Audrey and Zoe.

"What was that?" I ask as Ruby sits back down.

"It was the end of our friendship," Ruby says quietly. I turn to see Cher laughing with Audrey, and I think Ruby's right.

3:02 P.M.
LOCKERS

"Hey, Emma." I turn and find Connor smiling at me. Cher walks up and clears her throat. I ignore her but step out of her way, avoiding eye contact.

"Hey, one sec," I tell him. I grab my backpack and close my locker. "What's up?" We walk toward the doors side by side, close enough that our shoulders occasionally bump each other.

"What are you doing right now?" he asks.

"I don't know. Walking home?"

"Some of us are going to hang out at the park. You should come." We pause outside the school doors. Ruby is waiting for me at the corner. She waves when she sees us. "You can bring Ruby if you want," Connor adds.

Just then, Marie walks up to Ruby and gives her a hug. I sigh. "I can't. I have to watch my sister."

Connor shrugs. "Bring her, too."

"Ha! No way. She's so annoying." I roll my eyes for effect.

"Alright," he says. "Well... what about Friday after the field trip?"

Mom's off on Fridays and usually picks Marie up. I don't have plans, except to hang out with Ruby.

"Sure." I smile up at him. He checks over his shoulder that there are no teachers nearby and leans down to kiss me. *In front of everyone!* My cheeks are pleasantly warm when he pulls back.

"Cool. See you tomorrow." He jogs in the opposite direction.

"Emma!" Marie shouts from next to Ruby. Her jaw is practically on the ground, and her big brown eyes are wide. I blush, both from the kiss and Marie's reaction to it. Ruby raises her hands as if to say, "What did you expect me to do?" I groan as I walk over to them.

3:15 P.M.

"What's it worth to you?" Marie asks as we're walking home.

I sigh dramatically. "Whatever, Marie. If you're going to be a brat about it, go ahead and tell Mom."

"Can I hang out with you guys?" she asks eagerly.

"No."

"Come on!"

"No!"

"Just for an hour?" Marie stops in front of me, blocking the path.

Ruby lightly hip-bumps me. "What can it hurt, Em?"

"Fine," I snap. "Thirty minutes, and that's it."

"Yessss." Marie smiles and skips ahead of us. "Thirty minutes starts when we get home," she calls back.

"No kissing-talk while she's around," I whisper to Ruby. She mimes zipping her lips in response.

3:30 P.M.
BEDROOM

"Do you know what you're going to wear on Friday yet?" Ruby's staring into my closet, running her fingers down the sleeve of a fuzzy gray sweater.

"Ugh, no. I hate everything in there." I lie back on my pillow.

"What's Friday?" Marie pipes up from the end of my bed.

"Our field trip," Ruby says, walking back to us. She sits cross-legged on the floor.

"To where?" Marie slides down the bed to sit with Ruby.

"It's stupid," I say.

"It's to a health center. They're going to talk to us about periods and sex."

"Ew!" Marie says, wrinkling her nose.

"Exactly," Ruby and I say in unison.

Marie changes the subject. "What's it like kissing a boy?" She sits up taller and turns back to me, her eyes wide.

"Nope." I shake my head.

"Come on. What's the point of hanging out with you if you don't tell me the good stuff?"

I shrug and point to the door. "You can leave."

She turns to Ruby. "Have you kissed any boys?"

Ruby raises her eyebrows. "Nope. Boys are stupid." She pauses and then shivers. "No thanks."

Marie nods. "Totally... Okay, I'm gonna go. You guys are kind of boring." She gets up and walks out.

Ruby looks at me in surprise. "We are not boring!"

CHAPTER 24

The human body is a living miracle!

FRIDAY, MAY 14TH
9:57 A.M.

When we arrive at The Center for Health Education for our "field trip," the workers have us line up, boys and girls. We walk down the hallway and stop in front of two sets of big, brown doors. The boys go through the left door. The girls go through the right. We file in and take our seats. The room is really big; they could probably fit twenty more classes in here, but it's only one other group and us.

While we're waiting for the presenter, I notice a giant poster to my right with the reproductive organs of a man and a woman. I poke Ruby and point to the poster.

"Testes," I whisper. She snorts, and we both try to contain our giggles.

The lights dim a little, and a door opens at the back. A woman comes galloping out into the middle of the room and says into her microphone, "Good morning, ladies!" A few people mumble a good morning back.

"Aw, come on, girls. You can do better than that. Let's try it again. Good morning, ladies!" She puts her hand over her ear and leans toward us. I mumble, "Good morning." Ruby belts it out.

"Much better," the presenter says with a smile. She's probably around Ms. Stein's age—maybe in her thirties—but she's not as cool-looking as Ms. Stein. She's wearing jeans and a turtleneck, with an ugly purple and blue-striped scarf wrapped around her neck. Why would you wear a scarf with a turtleneck? Her hair is cut short, and she runs her hands through it before introducing herself.

"My name is Linda, and I am an education specialist here at The Center for Health Education. I am thrilled to have all of you here with me today to learn more about the way our bodies work. This is one of my favorite classes to teach because it's just us girls—no boys allowed.

"Now, one of the most important things to know about today's session is that there is nothing to be embarrassed about. The human body is a living miracle."

Ruby lightly bumps her shoulder against mine, and I smile. "Oh my God," I whisper.

"Before we get started, I need you girls to do something for me." Linda stops walking around the room and slowly pans her gaze across the audience. "I need you to say..." She pauses for dramatic effect. "Penis." She takes a step back and grins.

I freeze. Ruby freezes next to me. The room is silent. I think we're all in shock.

Linda puts her hands up and continues, "I know. I know. How embarrassing, right? But we're going to talk about boys' reproductive systems today, too, and I don't want you to feel weird about the word 'penis.'" She lets out an airy laugh. "I wish you could see your faces. You'd think I asked you to chop off your right arm.

"Stand up, girls. Let's do this. On the count of three, I want everyone to shout, *'penis!'* as loudly as you can."

It takes a few seconds, but everyone stands up. Most of the girls in the room are looking down at their feet or at the posters on the walls—anywhere except at Linda. I accidentally make eye contact with Cher, and we both look away quickly.

"Ready, girls?" Linda smiles and bounces on her toes. This is so weird. My cheeks are on fire. "One... Two..." I swallow. Why am I nervous about this? "Three!" Linda opens her arms wide and shouts, *"PENIS!"* She is exponentially louder than the rest of us.

Ms. Stein is sitting in the back with her face in her hands. Her shoulders are shaking. Is she laughing?

"Not bad, not bad," Linda says, "but I don't think I heard everybody. Don't worry about what the person next to you is thinking. She's as nervous as you are. Let it out. I promise it feels great."

No, it doesn't. It's embarrassing.

"You know what?" Ruby whispers. "It kind of does." She giggles and turns eagerly back to Linda.

"You're a weirdo," I tell her.

"Penissss," she whispers under her breath.

"Stopppp," I whine. We burst into giggles as Linda gives us another penis countdown. This time, I bellow as loudly as Ruby.

11:41 A.M.

Linda made us say "penis" about a hundred times during our presentation. By the end, I thought my face was going to boil off. Not only because of shouting about boy parts, but also because of all the talk about ovaries and menstruation. And intercourse and birth control. It was mortifying.

As we walk back toward the bus, Ruby links arms with me. "Well, that was informative."

I hip-bump her. "There's no denying that. But also super embarrassing. And gross. Can you imagine Mr. Jeffries doing it with his wife? Ugh, the pit stains!"

Ruby's mouth opens into a perfect circle. "Never. Speak of that. Again."

The boys' presentation must have finished before ours because they're already back on the bus when we get on. I was hoping to sit by Connor on the way to the restaurant, but he's all the way in the back with the other boys. I plop down next to Ruby instead.

As we drive, Ruby is rambling on about one of her cousins. "Are you listening, Emma?" She pokes me in the side.

"What? Yeah." I turn toward her as I hear the boys burst into raucous laughter behind us.

Ruby rolls her eyes. "You can talk to Connor when we get there. Pay attention to me." She pulls my arm and flings me back and forth a few times.

12:00 P.M.
CHUCK'S BURGERS

I take my time walking into the restaurant, hoping Connor will catch up with us. I pause to tie my shoe near the entrance. Ruby doesn't say anything, but she shakes her head slightly while she waits for me.

The place is full of booths with red, fake-leather seats and low-hanging lights above the table. It's almost romantic. My chest feels tight, and I hold my breath as I look over my shoulder. I feel a jolt of energy when I see a head of messy brown hair behind me.

"Hey, want to sit with us?" Connor asks. He glances at Hunter, behind him.

"Duh," Ruby says. She gently hip-bumps me, and we follow the boys toward the back of our reserved area. Connor and

Hunter sit across from each other, so I slide in next to Connor. Ruby gives me a sly smile as she bounces in next to Hunter.

12:28 P.M.

Of course, Audrey, Zoe, and Cher sit at the table right behind us. Cher has her back to us, so thankfully, I can't see her, but every time I hear her laugh, something in my chest tightens. Ruby and I lock eyes at a particularly loud burst of laughter from the three of them. She inhales deeply and closes her eyes for a second. She shakes it off and reaches for her lemonade, gulping it down.

I take a deep breath, too, and remind myself that I'm not putting energy into Cher anymore. I lightly kick Ruby under the table. She pushes her lemonade away, and I smile, trying to radiate my energy toward her instead. She smiles back gratefully.

Audrey kneels on the seat, peering over the booth. "Hunter," she whines, the same way I've heard her whine Connor's name. She's clearly trying to make him jealous.

Luckily, he doesn't seem to care. He holds my hand under the table the whole time we wait for our food.

2:49 P.M.

I wonder what the boys' presentation was about today. They didn't talk about periods. Did they? Oh my God. I hope not. I don't want Connor to know what's happening in my body. Well, okay, it's not happening in *my* body yet, but I think I might have had a cramp recently. So, that has to be a sign my period is coming, right? I cannot graduate eighth grade without having my period. Just, no.

CHAPTER 25

Are you kidding me, Emma?

FRIDAY, MAY 14TH
3:04 P.M.

"Hey, cutie." I feel Connor's arm around my shoulder before I see his face. My cheeks and my insides warm at his touch.

"Hey," Ruby says, winking at Connor. I shoot her a glare. Connor lets out a loud guffaw.

"Are you still coming to the park with us, Emma?" he asks.

"Yeah, we both are." I motion to Ruby, who links her arm through mine.

"Great. We'll meet you there. Okay?" Connor says, removing his arm from across my shoulders.

"Who's we? Who's all going?" Ruby asks.

"Um..." Connor thinks for a second, scratching his head. He looks like a dumb cartoon character—not that he's dumb. That's not what I mean. Just, it was a weird pose. Connor's actually pretty smart. He came up with the design for our rollercoaster.

He starts listing people. "Hunter, Marco, Liam, I think maybe Paul. Audrey, Zoe, Cher—"

"Audrey and Cher? Ughhhh," Ruby complains. She crosses her arms and rolls her eyes.

"We're not exactly friends with Audrey and Zoe—or Cher, anymore," I explain to Connor's bewildered expression.

Connor nods. "Gotcha. Well, you don't have to hang with them. I promise. I'll keep you entertained." He smiles and gives Ruby and me a hug at the same time, patting our backpacks with his long, tanned arms.

"Yeah, okay," I say, but Connor's already walking away.

"Are you insane, Emma?"

"Ruby, you heard him. We won't have to hang out with them."

"Yeah, maybe you won't, 'cause you'll be too busy making out with Connor. What am I supposed to do?" Ruby throws her arms into the air and starts walking in a circle.

Heat creeps up my neck, and I feel a tiny knot in the pit of my stomach. I put my arm out to stop Ruby's pacing. "We don't have to go if you don't want to, Ruby," I tell her quietly. I know it's the right thing to do, to choose my friend over a boy, but I really, *really* hope she says we can still go.

Ruby drops her head back and groans. "I know you don't mean that." She closes her eyes and lifts her head. When she opens them, her chocolatey-brown eyes lock on my sea-glass ones. She sighs. "Go ahead."

I start to bounce on my toes. *Thank God.* "Oh, Ruby, you are the best! You are such a good friend. No, you are the *best* best friend anyone could have!" I hop over and wrap her in the tightest hug possible.

Ruby pulls my arms from around her. "Are you kidding me, Emma?" She puts her hands on her hips and shakes her head, not looking at me.

"Wha—but, why?" I eventually spit out.

"Seriously? Are you really going to pick Connor over me?" Her eyes are wide, darting between my own.

"B-b-but, I offered—"

"Yeah," Ruby snorts, "you 'offered' not to go." She puts the word "offered" in air quotes. "But you didn't mean it. You still want to go, even though I'll feel super awkward the whole time. Like seriously, who do you think I'm actually going to talk to? I didn't even really want to go when you and I were going to be the only girls. And now, our arch-nemesis, her crony, and our former best friend are all going to be there, leaving me out and making nasty comments, all while you're off sucking face with Connor."

I know Ruby's right. I shouldn't go. But I want to so badly. I don't move. Instead, I stare at a crack in the sidewalk.

Ruby snorts again. In a low, quiet voice, she says, "I thought you were a better friend than this, Emma. Have fun at the park." Out of the corner of my eye, I see her turn and walk away. I continue to stare at the sidewalk for another few seconds.

I know I should call her name and try to stop her. I know I should go after her. But I don't. I turn and start walking toward the park.

8:58 P.M.
RUNNING

I pause to catch my breath on the corner four blocks from my house. My heart is racing, my throat is tight, and tears prickle the back of my eyes, but not because I sprinted the last eight blocks from the park.

I have two minutes to get home before Mom murders me. I take a deep gulp of air before I run off again.

9:02 P.M.

I come flying in the door. Mom is waiting for me.

"You're late." Her voice is dangerously quiet.

I give her a blank stare, blinking heavily.

"Don't blink at me," she snaps.

I shift my weight. What does she want me to do?

"Grounded." She puts her hand out. "Give me your phone."

I shrink into myself.

"Now, Emma."

"But—"

"*Now.*"

I shove the phone into her hand and run up the stairs, slamming my door with as much force as I can muster.

9:07 P.M.
BEDROOM

I was two minutes late. *Two* minutes!

Ugggghhhh! No phone, no friends. What am I going to do?

9:10 P.M.

Although, I guess it doesn't really matter since neither of my friends are speaking to me, and I'm pretty sure Connor doesn't like me anymore either.

I dramatically throw myself face-down onto my bed, and I start wailing. It's the hardest I've cried in a long time, and let's be honest, I've cried a lot.

Albus is trying to open the door. I can hear him jumping up and trying to fling down the handle. I ignore him.

9:11 P.M.

Except the sound is super annoying. I let out a long moan into my pillow and then drag myself up off the bed. I open the door to let the cat in, and I take this opportunity to slam my door nice and loud again. Albus darts under the bed at the sound of the door. I know Mom hears it, but she ignores me. This makes me even madder.

I pick up a notebook off my desk and start tearing pages out. I tear and rip until it's almost empty, and I'm standing in a pile of paper. This makes me furious for some reason. I pick up a handful of paper and grunt as I throw it at the wall. Each sheet slowly floats back to the floor.

I climb into my bed, fully clothed, lights still on. What have I done?

I am such an idiot. I knew I should have gone with Ruby, but I didn't. All because I wanted to kiss Connor again. I'm a horrible friend. No wonder I don't have any.

CHAPTER 26
I said NO!

FRIDAY, MAY 14TH
EARLIER TODAY

When I get to the park, Hunter calls out, "Hey, Captain! Your girl's here!"

Connor hops off the picnic table he's sitting on. My heart rate ticks up a few notches as I walk over to him and the other boys.

"Where's your sidekick?" he asks after giving me a quick hug.

I smile to myself, briefly distracted by how good Connor smells.

"Oh, her mom called her, and she had to go home. Family emergency," I lie.

"Bummer," Connor says, patting an empty space on top of one of the tables. I hop up, sliding my backpack off behind me. I nod. "I think Marco is kind of into her," he fake-whispers.

"Hey, man!" Marco says, gesturing around.

Connor gives a loud belly laugh, and I join in nervously. There's no way Ruby would like Marco. They were partnered up in math once, and she said he smelled like milk.

Marco and a couple of other guys start throwing a football around. Connor moves a little closer as he puts his arm around me. My cheeks are pleasantly warm as I feel the weight of his hand on my waist. I'm thinking, *How did I get so lucky?* when I notice three girls crossing the street in our direction.

It's Audrey, Cher, and Zoe. Audrey and Cher have their arms linked, and they're laughing about something together. Zoe's a few steps behind them, a forced smile on her face.

I shift in my spot on the table.

"What's wrong?" Connor asks.

"Um, nothing. It's just, you know, Cher and Audrey," I say quietly.

"Don't worry about them." He squeezes my waist. "Why don't we go over there for a while?" He motions behind us. "Then you don't even have to talk to them."

Connor doesn't wait for me to say anything. He grabs my hand and pulls me off the table. My heart starts pounding. Even though I've kissed Connor a couple of times already, I'm still nervous. We walk through the actual park area—past the swings, the monkey bars, and the slides—over to the picnic tables by the basketball courts. Connor hops up on top of the closest table and then offers me his hand to join him.

He doesn't waste any time and immediately leans in for a kiss. Everything is great, at first. I'm varying pressure, careful not to knock teeth. I even do a little nibble on his lip, which I think he likes because he moans a little. I pull back for a second, smiling at this beautiful boy in front of me. Connor licks his lips hungrily and pulls me back in.

I don't know how long we've been making out, but my jaw is starting to get tired. I try to pull away, but Connor puts his hand on the back of my head, moaning quietly. I don't like this. I pull away, harder this time, wiping my mouth on the back of my hand.

"What's wrong?" His ice-blue eyes lock on mine.

"Nothing," I say, smiling again. "I need some air." I force out a giggle.

Connor laughs. "Totally." He pauses for a second, watching the high schoolers play basketball at the courts across from us. "You know, you're a pretty great French kisser." He turns his head toward me and gives me a shy smile. "I really like hanging out with you, Emma."

I'm sure my face is as red as a tomato. All I can do is smile down at my feet. Connor bumps his shoulder against mine. "Do you want to go back over there?" He points his head back toward the boys, Audrey, Cher, and Zoe.

"Not really."

"Good." He smiles. "Me neither." Then he scoots closer and pulls my face toward his once again.

After a couple minutes of excellent kissing, I chance another nibble on Connor's lip. He must really like it because he makes that moaning sound again as he pulls me so close I'm practically sitting on top of him. He swings my legs over his lap and starts running his hand up and down my calf. Thank God I shaved my legs last night. After a couple of seconds of that, Connor moves his hand slowly up over my knee and starts rubbing my thigh. I try to play it cool and shift my weight a little, but he must think that means I like it. He lifts my skirt and slides his hand farther up my thigh.

My heart is pounding. I'm not even thinking about the kissing anymore, and I don't think Connor is either. Our mouths are just pressed together, occasionally opening and doing some tongue work. I feel Connor's hand start to slide farther up my leg, and I can't take it anymore. I pull away and put my hand over his.

"What's wrong? You don't like it?" Connor asks. Again, his eyes search mine, his forehead knit in concern.

I don't want him to think I'm a loser or some sort of baby, so I say, "Um, no, it's fine. It surprised me is all."

Connor lets out a sigh of relief. "Okay, good." He leans in for another kiss but stops suddenly. "Let me know if you want me to stop, okay?"

I smile and nod, warmth spreading through my chest. He's so sweet.

After more kissing and no further hand movement—thank God—we finally come up for air again. "I think we need to take a break," Connor says, laughing. "I can barely breathe."

We decide to go back over by everyone else. Connor promises I won't have to talk to my former best friend or Audrey and Zoe, and he holds my hand the entire time. Connor and I return to our picnic bench from before and listen to the story Hunter is telling.

All of a sudden, Audrey interrupts Hunter and shouts across the pavilion, "Connooooor!" dragging out his name in the annoying way only Audrey can. "Where've you been?"

"I was hanging out with Emma," he says calmly. He gives my hand a squeeze.

Audrey rolls her eyes. "Ew," she says under her breath. She turns to Cher, who gives her a high-five!

I blush. My throat tightens, and I feel a prickling behind my eyes. Obviously, Cher and I haven't been talking, but how could she do that to me? We make eye contact, and I swear, for a second, I see a little remorse in her eyes, but she quickly turns and bumps her shoulder against Audrey's.

I jump off the table and run back to the basketball courts. I hear Connor say something but can't tell what it is. I sit on the table where I was making out with Connor only a few minutes earlier. I felt so lucky then.

The sun is setting, giving everything an orange hue, and the guys who were playing basketball are gone now. I feel so alone. I put my face in my hands and start to cry. A minute later, I hear footsteps approaching, so I sit up and quickly wipe my eyes.

"Hey, Emma, you okay?" Connor asks quietly. He sits down next to me, just like earlier.

"Not really," I say honestly. A tear escapes and runs down my cheek.

"Don't pay any attention to Audrey," he says.

"It's hard not to. She's so loud," I say, sniffling.

Connor laughs. "True." He pauses for a second, looking at me. "Would some more French kissing make you feel better?"

I can't stand it anymore. "Only if you stop calling it that."

"Calling it what?" Connor asks, surprised.

"French kissing. I don't know. It weirds me out." I turn my head, looking at him sideways.

Connor laughs again. "You're such a goof." Then he leans in. He is really into it this time, pulling me closer and holding me more tightly than ever before. He's rubbing my back when all of a sudden, I feel his hand on my boob (or where my boob would be if I had any).

Without thinking, I let out a shocked, "Whoa," and I smack his hand away.

"What?" Connor says, looking dopey, his mouth hanging slightly open.

"I don't want to do that," I tell him quietly.

"Why not?" He scoots closer to me again.

"I just don't."

"Come on, you'll like it. I promise." He leans in again.

I push him away and shout, "I said *NO!*" Then I half-jump, half-fall off the table and run back to the pavilion. I grab my backpack, throw it over my shoulders, and keep running.

10:21 P.M.

I feel sick every time I think about Connor now. My stomach is in knots, and I wish I could talk to Ruby about it. I start crying again, this time silent tears streaming down my cheeks.

Albus hops up on my bed and snuggles in the crook of my legs. He starts to purr, and I feel a teeny, tiny bit better. At least *he* still likes me.

CHAPTER 27

Being fourteen is hard. Isn't it?

SUNDAY, MAY 16TH
9:10 A.M.

Days since I've spoken to Cher: 9
Days since I've spoken to Ruby: 2
Times I've kissed Connor: 6
Days since I've had my phone: 2
Times I've cried in the last forty-eight hours: 5

9:14 A.M.

Dad knocks on my door. "Come in," I mumble from under the covers. I've been hiding here since I woke up, like two hours ago. Mom's been ignoring me since Friday, so I've been avoiding going downstairs as much as possible. I don't know why she's so mad. It was two minutes! No one can hold a grudge like Mom.

"Hey, kiddo, you hungry?" Dad asks, sitting on the corner of my bed.

I poke my head out from under my covers. "A little."

"Why don't you come downstairs? Mom made pancakes."
He reaches out and shakes my leg.

"Is Mom still mad at me?"

Dad sighs. "Hiding up here isn't helping your case."

"She's scary when she's mad."

"I know." He stands up. "Get dressed and be downstairs in five minutes. Family breakfast."

9:30 A.M.
KITCHEN

Mom doesn't talk to me at breakfast, but she doesn't outright ignore me like she was yesterday. I'll call that progress.

When I offer to do the dishes after we eat—what a good, kind daughter I am—she smiles tightly and says, "Sure." I thought she'd be a little more appreciative, especially since pancakes make a lot of dirty, sticky dishes.

2:00 P.M.

Marie has her little boyfriend over. They're chasing each other around the house with Nerf guns. Oddly, it makes me want to cry. What is wrong with me? All I've been doing over the last two days is crying.

I walk down the stairs to get a snack, and Marie comes flying around the corner. She stops when she sees me, startled. Her little boyfriend—I think his name is Tony—comes up behind her, panting. They both stare at me. Marie elbows Tony. And then they both shoot their foam bullets at me.

And then I start crying. And I can't stop. Marie and Tony stare at me, sitting in a puddle of my own tears. Their eyes are wide, and they're both frozen in place.

"Mom?" Marie calls out feebly. "Something's wrong with Emma!"

BEDROOM

Mom sits next to me on my bed. I pick at an imaginary piece of lint to avoid looking at her.

"What's going on, Em?"

"Nothing."

"You burst into tears because Marie and Tony shot their Nerf guns at you. That doesn't sound like nothing."

I shrug, continuing to pick at my comforter.

She sighs. "I'm still not happy about what happened on Friday. As you get older, you need to be more responsible. I need to know I can trust you." She pauses. "Look at me, Emma." I reluctantly tear my eyes away from the blanket. I focus on her nose so I don't have to look her in the eye. "You can talk to me, even if I'm upset with you. You know that, right?"

I'm still staring at my mom's nose. I see a little red spot on the bridge. I gasp. "You have a zit on your nose!" I point accusingly at her.

"Ugh, yes. No need to point it out." She touches the tip of her nose delicately. "Same spot you had one a few weeks ago. Right?"

"Yeah... Oh my God! Am I still going to get zits when I'm old?"

"Hey, I'm not *that* old," Mom says defensively. Her cheeks turn a little pink.

"You're blushing," I say, and then I start to laugh, a maniacal belly laugh.

Mom stares at me for a second. "Emma, are you okay?" I nod but continue laughing. I don't know if it will ever stop. Mom starts laughing too. We're laughing so hard we both fall back onto my bed.

I don't know how long we're there, but eventually, we stop laughing and lie there quietly. Mom rolls over to face me. "I'm not going to force you to talk to me, Emma, but if you keep coming home late and slamming doors—"

I cut her off. "Cher isn't our friend anymore. She's hanging out with Audrey and Zoe now." I can feel everything bubbling up to the surface. It's like word-vomit. I can't stop talking. "Ruby and I got in a big fight yesterday. She didn't want to go to the park, but I went anyway, and now I feel like a horrible friend. And Connor definitely isn't going to like me anymore, but I'm not even sure I care because he has weird nails. And then I was late on Friday, and now I'm grounded and have no phone or anyone to talk to. It feels like my whole life is a mess, and I can't stop crying." Tears are streaming down my face again.

Mom rolls onto her back, and she's quiet for a second. We both stare at the ceiling. Finally, she says, "Being fourteen is hard. Isn't it?"

I sniffle. "Yeah."

8:08 P.M.

Mom and I talked for a long time in my bedroom. Then she took me for a milkshake, and we talked some more. Then we came home and watched a movie, and we didn't talk at all. I cried three more times, and Mom cried once.

It was a good day.

CHAPTER 28

I am not going to cry this time.

MONDAY, MAY 17TH
7:02 A.M.

I'm still lying in bed. I don't want to get up. If I get up, that means I have to go to school, and I don't want to go to school. I don't want to see Connor. I don't want to see Cher. I don't want to see Audrey. But I do want to see Ruby. I miss her, and I need my friend back. As cool as Mom was yesterday, I don't want to be the loser who only hangs out with her mom.

I throw the covers off of me, and Albus scurries away. I follow suit and hop out of bed.

7:31 A.M.

"Wish me luck," I say to Mom. I grab my backpack and walk toward the door.

"Are you sure you don't want a ride, Em?"

"Yes. I want to talk to Ruby." I stand up a little taller, but at the same time, my heart is racing. I'm so nervous. I don't know if Ruby's still mad at me because even though we hung out all day yesterday, Mom won't give me my phone back. Apparently, being without my phone for a week will make me more responsible...

7:35 A.M.
OUTSIDE RUBY'S HOUSE
There's no way Ruby left before me. I have a sneaking suspicion she's inside, waiting for me to leave. But I'm not going to.
Unless it gets so late that I see Mom drive by.

7:58 A.M.
Ruby is so stubborn. I saw her peek out the window five minutes ago, but she still hasn't come out. And I'm so bored. I can't even go on my phone, so all I can do is stand here and look at nature.

8:05 A.M.
Mom's car turns the corner. I let out a defeated sigh and wave her down. As I close the door of the backseat, Ruby runs out of her house and down the street.

"What the—" Mom starts to say. Before I can buckle my seat belt, Mom takes off to catch up to Ruby.

"Ruby! Get in the car. You're going to be late," Mom yells out Marie's window.

"No... I'll... be... fine..." Ruby huffs.

Mom continues to drive slowly next to her until Ruby finally gives up. She takes a deep breath and walks over to the car. She gets in the backseat and stares straight ahead.

"Hi," I say quietly.

Ruby rolls her eyes and looks out the window in response. I don't say anything else. I try to ignore the prickling behind my eyes.

8:37 A.M.
ENGLISH

Ms. Stein is rambling on about symbolism or metaphors or something, but I can't concentrate. All I want to do is curl up into a ball and cry.

When we got to school, Ruby immediately sped off. She stood at the entrance with her back to me until we could go in. Connor was standing around with Hunter, Marco, and the rest of the boys. He didn't even look my way, which was actually a relief. Cher was, of course, with Audrey and Zoe, whispering and giggling menacingly. Probably about me.

I stare down at the story in front of me, but I'm not actually reading any of the words.

What am I going to do?

LUNCH

My heart is racing as I walk into the lunchroom. I'm going to try again to make up with Ruby. I can't take it anymore. She's sitting at our usual table, seemingly unbothered by the fact that she's alone. She's an only child; I guess she's kind of used to it.

I cautiously put my lunch down and stand across from her for a second.

She looks up at me, her eyebrows raised. "Are you going to sit down or stand there like a weirdo?"

I can't help but smile a little as I pull my chair out.

"Stop staring at me," Ruby says.

"Sorry."

"Why didn't you answer any of my texts?" Ruby demands.

"My mom took my phone away."

"Why?"

"Because I was late on Friday."

"Well, that was stupid."

"I know."

"I'm still mad at you."

"Okay. I'm kind of mad at me, too."

"Why?"

I pull out my sandwich and unwrap it. I take a bite. Ruby stares at me.

"Why are you mad at yourself, Emma?" Ruby's face softens. She can tell something happened.

Oh, no. I feel the prickle behind my eyes again. Why, *why* must I be such a freaking baby? I stare at my sandwich because if I open my mouth to start talking, I'm afraid I'll start bawling. Ruby gets up and comes over to sit next to me. She puts her arm around my shoulder.

"Is it Connor?"

I nod.

"What. Did. He. Do?" Ruby asks through clenched teeth.

"It's not just him, Rubs. It's everything. All weekend I felt so alone." My voice cracks. I take a deep breath. "It's Connor, and Cher, and then... you. I couldn't even talk to you. And I knew it was all my fault. It was horrible." There's no stopping them at this point. Tears are streaming down my face. I take another deep, shuddering breath.

"Come on. Bathroom." Ruby pulls me up and shuffles me out of the lunchroom. Once we're in there—we had no problem getting a pass from Mr. Jeffries. He's terrified of girls crying—I let it all out. I tell Ruby about everything that happened with Connor. I tell her how lonely I felt without her all weekend. I tell her how hurt I am that Cher doesn't want to be our friend anymore. I tell her that I can't seem to stop crying, ever.

She lets me talk and talk and talk, without ever interrupting me, even though I know she wanted to a couple times. When I finish, she gives me a big, long hug.

"I'm not mad at you anymore," she says into my ear.

"You should be," I whisper.

"You're not wrong." She pauses for a second and steps out of our embrace. "It's always been the two of us, Em. You can't start picking people over me. I know you were having all the feels for Connor, but sometimes you have to remember that other people are outside of that bubble. People who have feelings too."

It hurts to hear, but I know she says it out of love and because she doesn't want me to be a crappy friend. "You're right, Rubs. I'm so sorry."

She smiles and takes a step forward, putting her hands on either side of my face. "If you ever do that to me again, I will kick. Your. Ass." I let out a snort, but Ruby doesn't let go. "But. I will always be your friend, Emma."

We hug again for a long time. I'm so happy to have my friend back.

"I have to pee," I say. Ruby gives me an extra squeeze before she lets go. "Hey, don't squeeze it out of me." Ruby laughs. She turns to check her hair in the mirror. In the stall, I go about my business, but before I stand up, I notice something.

"Ruby..." I say slowly.

"Yeah?" she says. "Hurry up! We have like five minutes before the bell rings, and I have Oreos that cannot be wasted."

"Ruby," I say again, seriously.

"What, Emma?"

"I think..." I'm not sure how to say it. "I think I got my period."

Ruby gasps. "Oh my God! Really? Oh my God, Emma! Yay!" She starts jumping up and down and clapping. "Welcome to womanhood, my beautiful friend!"

"Ruby." She doesn't hear me. She's talking about pads and tampons, and maybe our cycles will sync up. "Ruby!" I shout.

She freezes right in front of my stall. "Yeah?"

"Can you go get me a pad from the nurse?" I hold in the giggle threatening to escape.

"Oh my God. I'm such an idiot. Of course. I'll be right back." She runs out the door.

I'm alone, staring at the gray door in front of me. The giggle escapes. The thought of me, sitting alone in the school bathroom with my period, is too much.

The door opens, and I stop laughing. I'm about to call out Ruby's name when I hear a familiar voice: Cher's. "So, come on. Tell me everything. What did he say?" she squeals.

Without thinking, I lift my feet up off the ground. I put them on the back of the stall, so it looks like it's empty.

Audrey laughs. "I already told you, there's not much to tell." She sounds so full of herself. I peek out the gap in the stall and see a sliver of Audrey, tossing her long, blond hair behind her shoulders; she reaches up and tousles the top. She turns, and I lean back onto the toilet. I silently pray that Ruby doesn't come barging in. What are they talking about? Where is Zoe?

"Well..." Audrey drags it out for a couple seconds. This is infuriating. "Like I said, I texted him Saturday, but he didn't respond."

Who is the "he" Audrey texted?

"So, I texted him again on Sunday, and I was like, 'Hey, way to ignore me yesterday,' and he was like, 'Oh, sorry. I didn't see your text.'"

I hear Cher make a disbelieving noise, but Audrey doesn't seem to notice. Cher says, "Okay, and then..."

"Well, I was trying to play it cool, so we went back and forth, talking, for a while—did you know, both of our favorite animals are polar bears? Then finally, I was like, 'So what do you think of Cher?'" Cher doesn't say anything. I'm still trying to keep my legs up on the stall door, but they're getting tired, and Ruby is going to be back any second. Spit it out, Audrey. "And he was like, 'What do you mean?' So I said, 'Oh, come on, Connor—'"

I don't hear anything after that. It's like I have earplugs in; I know there are noises around me, but I can't make out what they are. My vision blurs. But I am not going to cry this time. Instead, I quietly put my feet down, fold up some toilet paper and put it in my underwear, stand up, and flush the toilet. Audrey and Cher go silent. I take a deep breath and open the door.

CHAPTER 29

You what?

MONDAY, MAY 17TH
12:35 P.M.

Oh. My. God. I strut out of the bathroom. Ruby comes flying around the corner, and we almost collide.

"What took you so long?" I demand.

"The nurse was interrogating me." Ruby rolls her eyes. "Here." She tries to hand me a pad the size of the *Titanic*.

I don't take it. "What? No."

Ruby chuckles. "I know. It wouldn't even fit in my pocket." She starts walking toward the bathroom.

I grab her arm. "Nope. Audrey and Cher are in there." I lower my voice. "And I just called Cher a bitch."

"You *what?*" Ruby screams.

"Girls!" Mrs. Short comes out of her classroom. "Why am I always finding you in the hallway? Aren't you supposed to be outside right now?"

"Yes, we're going, Mrs. Short. Sorry," Ruby says, pulling me down the hallway.

"Sorry." I wave, following Ruby. Mrs. Short walks back into her classroom, shaking her head. We speed walk down the hallway and out the doors, and then we run over to the parking lot where the middle school kids have break. Ruby and I find an unbroken parking bumper and sit down.

Ruby realizes she's still holding the giant pad. "Ah! What should I do with this?"

I giggle, wondering if anyone saw us walking around with this massive feminine product. It's too funny to even be embarrassed. "I don't know. Throw it out?"

Ruby hops up and runs over to the garbage can near the door, her arm fully extended like she's holding something rancid. She tosses it, wipes her hands on her skirt, and races back over to me, smiling. She plops back down on the bumper with a quiet, "Oof," and then turns to me, her brown eyes searching mine. "What has gotten into you, Emma Bishop? You get your period, and now you're some sort of daredevil?"

I smile. "I know. I don't know what I was thinking."

Ruby reaches out and shakes me by my shoulders. "What. Happened?"

I explain how Cher and Audrey came in, and I continued to hide. When I tell her about the conversation I heard, her jaw drops open. "No," she says.

"Yes." I nod solemnly. "I was fuming. I can't believe that Cher would do that to me, even if we're not friends anymore." Ruby shakes her head. "So, I walked out there, and they were both staring at me.

"Audrey asked if I'd been there the whole time, eavesdropping on them, but I ignored her. I walked over to the sink and washed my hands without saying anything. As I was about to walk out the door, I turned back, looked Cher straight in the face, and said, 'Bitch.'"

I don't know why, but I am beaming.

"Did she say anything back?" Ruby asks.

I shake my head. "No. She stared at me like a deer in the headlights. She didn't say anything the entire time I was out there."

"What about Audrey?"

"Nope." I shrug.

"How did it feel?"

"Ruby, it felt *so* good!" I bump her shoulder, and we both start laughing.

3:11 P.M.
WALKING HOME

What a weird day. Ruby and I have our arms linked as we walk down the street, discussing the day's events. Obviously, I didn't speak to Audrey or Cher the rest of the day, and I avoided Connor completely, too. I don't even care if he doesn't like me anymore because I don't like him. The thought of him makes my stomach churn. I don't want to be with someone who thinks they can do whatever they want. Or someone who says, "French kissing." Or has weird fingernails.

"Honestly, Emma, that could have gone so much worse," Ruby says as we cross the street. "Connor is a pig. Did you tell your mom what happened?"

"Sort of... I told her that we kissed, but he didn't ask to be my boyfriend. I also told her about 'French kissing.' She thought it was weird too. But I didn't tell her about the whole boob thing."

Ruby shudders dramatically. "The whole thing gives me the heebie-jeebies."

"I know. Me too." We're both quiet for a second. "I guess my mom was right."

"What do you mean?"

"She's given me a couple motherly talks about not doing things I'm uncomfortable with. You know, 'It's okay to say no' and 'You don't have to do anything you don't want to.'"

"Your mom is a smart lady," Ruby says.

I nod, and we continue walking home arm in arm.

CHAPTER 30

Maybe you'll get boobs now.

4:47 P.M.
BEDROOM

I hear Mom in the hallway and call out, "Mom? Can you come in here?"

Mom comes storming in. "What's wrong?" Her eyes dart around my room. She runs over and puts her hand on my forehead. "Are you sick?"

I push her hand away. "What? No."

"Oh." Mom puts her hands on her hips. "Well, I assumed something must be wrong if you're calling me into your bedroom."

I roll my eyes but also give her a small smile. "Whatever." I have butterflies in my stomach. I fiddle with the blanket in my lap and clear my throat. "Um..." I don't know why I'm nervous.

Mom sits down on the edge of the bed. "What is it, honey?" Her voice oozes with worry.

"It's nothing bad," I assure her. "I, uh, got my period at school today." My cheeks are already warm, but they catch on fire when Mom starts screaming.

"Oh, Emma! Emma! I'm so proud of you!" She stands up and looks around the room like she doesn't know where to go. "This is so exciting." She walks toward the door and yells, "Roy! Guess what?"

I leap from my spot on the bed and pull her out of the doorway. *"Mom!* What is wrong with you? Dad doesn't need to know!"

She rolls her eyes but shouts down the hall, "Never mind." Dad is apparently unconcerned by the shouting, but unfortunately, Marie is not. She comes running into my bedroom.

"What's going on?" she asks, her head turning between Mom and me. She looks around my bedroom for any clues.

"Emma got her period," Mom whispers loudly into Marie's ear.

"Gross," Marie says, turning to leave. Before she does, though, she pauses in the doorway. "Maybe you'll get boobs now." She shrugs and walks down the hall.

Mom bursts into laughter, but Marie has a point. I walk over to the mirror and pull my shirt flat against my chest. Oh my God. They're definitely bigger. They're about the size of mosquito bites, but I'll take what I can get.

"Can we go to the mall?" I ask sweetly, casually pushing my chest out ever so slightly. "I think I need a new bra." Mom's eyes are shining. "Mom. Don't. Do not cry."

She puts her hands up in surrender. "I won't. I won't." She turns to leave.

"Wait, Mom. Mall?"

With a smile, she nods and then walks out. I hear her close the door to her bedroom a couple of seconds later. She definitely went in there to cry.

Well, at least I know where I got my crying gene from.

5:34 P.M.

MALL

Mom insists we start at the department store. "They have really nice bras that are much more reasonably priced." But when I hear department store, I think of old ladies and giant bra straps. The bra department is at the front of the store, which is totally embarrassing. Anyone can see you shopping for bras as soon as they walk in the door. I walk confidently over to a row of lacy bras that could fit on my head. I start rifling through, trying to find an "A" cup.

"Emma," Mom calls out loudly. She raises her eyebrows at me. "Seriously?" I shrug, turning away. "Come over here." She waves me over to the Juniors' bra section, which, thank the Lord, is not in the direct eye line of every single person entering the store.

We find a couple of really cute bras—my favorite is a turquoise-blue one with little bows on each of the straps. Mom continues to look, and I head toward the fitting room. As I get closer, I hear people yelling.

A girl shouts, "Just get out, Mom! I don't need your help. God, you're so annoying." For the second time today, I recognize the voice. It's Cher.

Cher's mom's voice is shrill when she says, "Don't you dare talk to me like that. You're embarrassing yourself and me. Get dressed. We're leaving. *Now!*"

The door slams on the fitting room. "Whatever. I'm not going to dinner at Jerry's."

"You are. And you're going to be nice about it." Cher's mom uses that dangerously quiet voice only moms have.

I slowly back out of the fitting room, but Cher's mom comes storming out, almost trampling me. She stops when she sees me and runs her hand through her blond hair—two things Cher must have inherited from her.

"Oh, hello, Emma." Her voice drips with a sweetness I know she's faking. She touches an expensive-looking but kind of ugly necklace around her neck. She glances back toward the fitting rooms. "How are you, sweetie? Is your mom here?" She doesn't wait for me to answer and shuffles past. She sees my mom and immediately turns to walk in the other direction. "Forgot something I needed over here," she explains quickly. "Be sure and tell your mom I said 'Hi,' okay?"

"Sure Mrs.—" I stop myself before I finish. I'm never sure what I'm supposed to call Cher's mom, since she's divorced. Do I call her Mrs. Doyle? Ms. Doyle? Do you get your old name back if you're divorced? "Sure," I repeat. I give her a small smile and start back toward my mom.

"How'd it go, Emma?" Mom has three more bras in her hands now.

"Oh, um…" I am not going in that fitting room with Cher still in there. I know what she's like when she fights with her mom, and it is not pretty. My heart lurches briefly. I also know how upset Cher gets when she and her mom are like this. My compassion doesn't last, though. She can talk about it with her new BFF, Audrey.

"Going now," I explain, pointing behind me. I try to find an alternative fitting room, but the nearest is in the men's section. I decide it would be weird to try on bras there. I drag my feet back to the original fitting room. I creep in, poking my head around the corner first to check if Cher is still in there. She is. I hear her sniffle. I walk loudly into the stall on the end, and I bang the door shut so she knows she's not alone. The sniffling stops, and I can hear her shuffling around. I pretend to be an unknowing stranger and try my bras on (facing away from the door, in case any creepers peer through the cracks). Cher leaves the dressing room, and I let out a sigh of relief and drop the straps I'm trying to attach.

I have that icky feeling again. Should I have told her it was me?

No. Don't be a fool, Emma. Cher's the one who betrayed Ruby and me and decided she wanted to be best friends with our mortal enemy. Not to mention the whole Connor thing from earlier today. When I remember that, my blood starts to boil, and I know I made the right choice by not saying anything.

I pick the straps up and get them hooked on the first try. Pleased, I turn and admire myself in the turquoise bra. It's cute, comfortable, and padded—what more could I ask for?

9:10 P.M.
BED

I got three new bras today—the turquoise one and two more "functional" bras, as Mom put it. I can't wait to wear them.

I feel a little weird. Like, I have my period now, and my boobs are *finally* growing. But also, I don't know, I have this unsettled feeling in my stomach. It's almost like when you're little and you have your first sleepover. You're really excited to stay up all night with your friend, but you're also kind of homesick. That's how I feel right now.

9:22 P.M.

I also keep thinking about Cher and the fight I heard with her mom. Should I say something to her?

9:24 P.M.

No. Obviously, she doesn't care about me anymore, so why should I care about her? She's always known how much I liked Connor. It's not like it was a secret.

And for the record, I knew something was off from the beginning. When Connor and I first started talking is when she started acting weird. Then she totally ditched Ruby and me. And now she's stabbing me in the back. Obviously, boys are more important to her than friendship.

9:27 P.M.
Not that I even care about Connor specifically. I don't want to be with him. I don't even want to see him or his weird fingernails.

Plus, the whole boob thing. Why do boys want to touch boobs, anyway? All Connor did was put his hand on my chest, basically. Why is that fun? Do they play with them? If there was more there, would he have jiggled them or something? I reach my hand under the blanket and cup my itty-bitty bits with my hand. There's not really enough to jiggle them. I move my hand back and forth, kind of rubbing my left boob.

I don't get it.

CHAPTER 31

What did I just see?

FRIDAY, MAY 21ST
4:02 P.M.
BEDROOM

Ruby and I are hanging out in my bedroom, watching Celsius music videos. I hear the door open downstairs.

"Mom?" I call out.

"Mrs. Bishop?" Ruby bellows.

I elbow her. "Ow, that was right in my ear."

"You'll survive."

"If you want to talk to me, you'll have to come down here, Emma," Mom calls up. "You too, Ruby," she adds.

4:03 P.M.
KITCHEN

Ruby and I come flying into the kitchen. Mom and her sea-glass eyes look us up and down suspiciously. "What do you want?"

"How do you know—" Ruby starts to say, but Mom raises her hand and cuts her off.

"I know these things. What is it?" She looks from me to Ruby, raising her eyebrows skeptically.

"Can we go ice skating tonight?" Ruby folds her hands in front of her chest like she's praying. "Everyone is going. It's their monthly open skate. We got a flyer at school this week."

"Well, I'm not in charge of you, Ruby. Did you ask your own mother?"

She nods and bounces up and down on her toes.

"Please, Mom? I've been so helpful this week, and—"

Ruby cuts me off this time, "And she's a woman now." Ruby winks and continues, "Which means she's more responsible and won't be late."

Mom rolls her eyes. "It's May. Who goes ice skating in May?"

"Everyone," I whine.

"It's an indoor rink, Mrs. Bishop," Ruby says knowledgeably.

Mom looks at me for a second; she lets a small smile creep across her face. "Okay, you can go." She leaves the room, and Ruby and I dance around the kitchen.

Mom comes back in a minute later. She holds out her hand. "I guess you'll be needing this, then." It's my phone. Before she can change her mind, I snatch it out of her hand and shriek with delight.

I grab Ruby's hands, and we jump around and dance in circles. Mom leaves again, shaking her head. She calls back over her shoulder, "Nine o'clock, Emma. Not a second later. I'd suggest walking in that door at 8:55."

4:45 P.M.
RUBY'S BEDROOM

Ruby pulls a leather skirt out of her closet. "What about this?"

"Ruby. We're going *ice skating.*"

"It's in—"

"I know, but it's still cold in there. Because, you know, ice?" I explain slowly.

Ruby harrumphs and turns back to her closet. I flick the teddy bear on my lap in the nose and then toss him over my shoulder to join the other twenty or so behind me. I flip over onto my stomach, patiently waiting for Ruby to find something for me to wear.

While she does, I scroll through my texts. It feels like I've been without my phone *forever*. Pretty much all the texts I had were from Ruby, both from when she was mad at me and when she would forget I didn't have my phone.

> Ruby: Oh, shoot. I forgot you don't have your phone. Again.
>
> Ruby: Sorry lol.

Unsurprisingly, based on our complete and utter avoidance of each other at school this week, there were no messages from Connor. But honestly, it feels like closure. It confirms what I've been thinking. Whatever was going on between us is over now.

A weight has been lifted off my shoulders. I feel light and happy. We're going to have fun tonight. I have my phone back, and no one is going to jiggle my boob. Unless I tell them they can.

6:08 P.M.
ICE RINK

Ruby and I walk in, and the place is packed. *Everyone* is here. People are standing in clusters along the walls, sitting on the benches tying up skates, and claiming tables at the food station. We pay and grab a locker to put our stuff in before putting on our skates.

I'm so glad Georgia helped me with my sea-glass eye makeup. She did it in about five seconds. It would have taken me at least six tries to put mascara on without poking myself in the eye.

I wore black jeans with a white t-shirt and a really cool, very unlike me, leather jacket that used to be Georgia's. I feel like a biker chick, like no one is going to mess with me tonight. Ruby ended up wearing the leather skirt with a red long-sleeve shirt.

"You look like you're going to a Christmas party," I told her.

"I look fabulous," she retorted.

We make our way out onto the ice and start skating around the rink in a big loop, checking out who else is here. Laney Lindt is shuffling around against the wall; Alejandra is in the middle with two girls I don't recognize, and they're all twirling like ice-ballerinas; Connor and Hunter are zipping past everyone else, randomly skidding the ice to stop and trip each other; and Cher, Audrey, and Zoe are sitting in the stands judging everyone beneath them. Audrey leans over and whispers something behind her hand to Cher. Cher leans forward and whispers in Zoe's ear. All three of them burst into giggles, covering their mouths. A flicker of annoyance passes through my brain, but I shake it off.

Ruby starts skating backward. I try to imitate her, but I can't seem to figure it out.

Alejandra comes gliding over, her long, dark hair in a sleek ponytail. "Bishop, you need some work," she says disdainfully.

"Hey, I'm as graceful as a swan."

"Ha!" both Ruby and Alejandra guffaw.

"Want to come skate with us?" Alejandra motions to the two girls still twirling in the middle of the rink. "I can try to help you look like less of a fool. I've been skating since I was like three."

I turn to Ruby, who nods enthusiastically.

7:12 P.M.

FOOD STATION TABLES

We decide to take a break from skating and claim a table on the outskirts of the food area with Alejandra and her friends. Ruby gets in line for a soft pretzel with cheese, and I go to the vending machines to get us a pop. When I turn the corner, I find Cher leaning up against a machine. She's turned away from me, facing the wall, and her shoulders are just barely shaking. She's crying. I start to back away, but I know Ruby will yell at me if I don't bring her a pop, so I walk up to the machine, ignoring my former friend crying three feet away from me.

When she hears me walk up, Cher turns and rolls her eyes. "Leave me alone, Emma," she mumbles.

I don't really know what to do. I ignore her and put my money in the machine. Cher hasn't moved, so I sneak another glance. She's wiping her eyes.

Without knowing it's going to come out of my mouth, I ask, "What's wrong?"

Cher turns over her shoulder and narrows her eyes. "Why do you care?"

I hate to say that she's right, but Cher's right. Why *do* I care? I shrug and push the button for an orange pop. Cher takes a deep breath and walks past me, lightly brushing my shoulder. I watch her walk out into the crowd.

Ruby reaches for the pop before I can even sit down at the table. She takes a big chug of it and lets out a satisfied, "Ahhh." She's talking to the other girls about music. I decide not to tell her about Cher yet.

I take a bite of pretzel and scan the area for Cher. I think she must have gone back into the rink until a golden glint catches my eye. Cher's blond ponytail bounces as she walks toward Audrey and Zoe. She sits down next to Zoe and forces a smile. Audrey continues talking about whatever stupid thing she's talking about, and Cher looks to the side and rolls her eyes. Audrey is too interested in her own story to notice, but I do.

"What are you staring at?" Alejandra asks, waving her hand in front of my face.

I shake my head. "Nothing. I must have been spacing out."

8:02 P.M.

SKATING AGAIN

We go back out on the ice, and Alejandra and her friends start twirling some more. Ruby and I skate slowly around them, ooh-ing and ahh-ing and clapping. I had no idea Alejandra was an ice skater or that she and Ruby had so much in common (they both love orange pop, collect stuffed animals, and have an aunt named Jess), which we discovered during our snack break.

As we skate in circles, I find myself looking for Cher again, which is stupid because I don't even care what's going on with her. She has new friends she can talk to now.

Cher, Audrey, and Zoe are back in the bleachers. Why come ice skating if you're not actually going to skate? Connor and Hunter walk up to the three of them. Audrey pushes Zoe away, so Connor can sit down next to her. He does. And then he puts his arm around her.

My mouth drops open, but I'm not sure why because I'm not actually surprised. It's Audrey, come on. What surprises me is that Cher's face gets red. Like, tomato red, like mine does.

I elbow Ruby in the ribs. "Ow! What was that for?" She unlinks her arm from mine and rubs her side. I look pointedly up at the bleachers. Ruby follows my gaze, scanning the crowd. I know she sees what I see because she narrows her eyes and makes a smacking noise.

"I need to go to the bathroom," I say.

"Thanks for the announcement," Alejandra says in the middle of a fancy spin.

I pull Ruby's arm to follow me.

8:10 P.M.
BATHROOM

Once we check the stalls to make sure we're alone, Ruby says, "What did I just see?"

"I know," is all I say. I lean back against the sink.

"Was Cher..." Ruby appears to be at a loss for words, which is quite possibly a first. She throws up her arms.

"Red?" I finish.

Ruby turns to me, eyes wide. "Making sad, googly eyes at Connor?"

"That too."

"Are you mad?" Ruby comes to lean against the sink next to me.

I think about it for a second. I mean, yes, I'm mad. I'm fuming. In the mirror, my cheeks match the color of Ruby's shirt. But also, I'm not. I already heard Cher and Audrey talking about Connor in the bathroom the other day. Plus, I don't even like Connor anymore. He has weird fingernails and uses the term French kissing. But on a third hand, if I had one, the betrayal still stings.

Before I can figure out how to explain my conflicting feelings to Ruby, the bathroom door opens. A blond ponytail flies past us and into the last stall, slamming the door shut. We can hear sniffling and a very quiet whimper. Ruby and I look at each other. Whoever is in the stall is crying. And I think I know who it is.

Ruby and I stand there, silent and unmoving. Another sniffle comes from the stall, and then a loud bang against the door. It creaks open, and she whispers a quiet curse.

I take a couple of cautious steps toward the stall. "Cher?"

She must have kicked the door. Cher is leaning back on the toilet, her legs stretched out in front of her. Her cheeks are blotchy, and she swipes at them as I push the door open further. Ruby strides up behind me. I can feel the energy radiating off of her.

"Are you okay?" I venture.

Cher snorts and shakes her head. Obviously, she's not okay, but what else am I supposed to say? Cher looks up at the ceiling and mumbles something.

"Sorry, didn't catch that," Ruby says loudly.

Cher darts her eyes at us and then back at the ceiling again. "I didn't mean to like him."

"Did you mean to like Audrey?" Ruby snaps back.

Cher stares at her feet. A tear streaks her flushed cheeks.

I don't know what to say. I look at Cher, sitting on the toilet. A giggle escapes. I try to seal my lips shut, but I can feel more giggles bubbling in my stomach. I clear my throat in an attempt to stop it. Cher raises an eyebrow. I try to raise one back at her. She drops her eyebrow and makes a face.

And then it starts. At first it's giggles, but after a couple of seconds, I am full-on belly laughing. Cher looks at me like I've lost my mind. Once I'm laughing, really laughing, Ruby joins in. Cher still sits on the toilet staring at us in disbelief.

She stands up, puts her hands on her hips, and shouts, "*Why* are you laughing?"

This only makes us laugh harder. Ruby puts her arm around my shoulder and leans on me for support. Cher plops back down onto the toilet in a huff. "Can you two stop?" she says quietly.

Suddenly my giggles are gone. Next to me, Ruby stands up on her own and takes a deep breath in.

"It's just... you, sitting on a toilet, crying. I'm usually the one crying." I offer a tentative smile.

Cher looks down at her feet again as another tear slides down her cheek. She uses the back of her hand to wipe it away. I guess it doesn't seem so funny anymore.

"Do you want to go?" I ask.

Cher jerks her head up. She looks from me to Ruby a couple of times. When no one says anything, Cher says, "Me? Are you talking to me?"

I shrug. "Ruby's spending the night. Do you want to come?"

Cher stands up and pushes past us. She grabs a paper towel, wets it with some water, and holds it under each of her eyes for a second. Ruby and I watch in silence. Finally, Cher pulls her shoulders back, takes a deep breath, and says, "Yes." Then she comes charging over to wrap Ruby and me in a tight hug.

CHAPTER 32

Because that's what real friendship is.

8:24 P.M.

I call Mom immediately to come pick us up. She's surprised but doesn't ask any questions.

Ruby and Cher sit on a bench at the front. Cher doesn't want to see anyone. I run back to the lockers to grab our stuff and Cher's. Ruby and I are changing out of our skates when all of a sudden, Alejandra pops into my brain.

"Ruby! Alejandra is going to think we're so rude. We went to the bathroom and never came back." I hop up. "I'll run out there and tell her we're leaving."

Ruby waves her hand at me. "I already texted her." I tilt my head to the side, confused. "She gave me her number when we got snacks." Ruby shrugs. "She's cool."

I nod in agreement, feeling relieved.

After we return our skates, the three of us head out the door.

8:50 P.M.

BEDROOM

Mom was even more surprised when Cher crawled into the backseat after Ruby. She made a little gasping noise and raised an eyebrow at me. Once again, I raised one back. She didn't say anything but smiled softly.

When we get to our house, Ruby, Cher, and I go straight up to my bedroom. We change into pajamas and sit cross-legged on my bed. No one says anything.

"So…" Ruby says, looking from me to Cher. "Should we talk?"

"Yes," I declare. Ruby and I both look at Cher expectantly. She nods slowly. "I don't really know what to say," she starts.

Ruby leans forward. "Why'd you ditch us for Audrey?" She doesn't say it in a mean way, more like stating a fact.

Cher fiddles with the bottom of the pajama pants I lent her. She rubs her finger over one of the kitties that adorn them like she's petting it. "I don't know—"

"Stop saying 'I don't know!'" Ruby interrupts.

Cher throws her hands up. "Well, I don't. It wasn't like I woke up one morning and thought, *Oh, I'm going to become friends with Audrey and ditch Ruby and Emma.* It just kind of… happened."

Ruby rolls her eyes. I speak up before she can say anything. "Okay, let's not fight." I put my arms out between them and rest a hand on each of their knees. I pause, thinking. "Were you mad at us?" I ask Cher.

She shakes her head, her blond ponytail gently swinging behind her. She continues to stare at the kitties on the pajamas. When she looks up, her blue eyes are watery. "I was jealous."

"Of what?" I ask.

Cher levels her gaze on me. "You," she whispers.

Even though I suspected this, I find it hard to believe now that I'm hearing it out loud. Cher was jealous of *me.* How is that even possible? Cher is smart, beautiful, funny, and confident; she has boobs and long, luscious hair; her makeup is always perfect, and she has the best clothes.

I realize I'm staring. I blink.

"Because of Connor, obviously," Ruby chimes in. "Right?"

"Sort of." Cher rubs the kitties on the pajamas again. "I mean, yeah." She pauses to glance up at me and then Ruby. "I tried not to be, honestly, but it would boil up in me, and I would get kind of mad, or sad, or whatever, and then Audrey was there, and she hated that he liked you, Em, and it was easy to complain to her."

I get a small amount of satisfaction that Audrey was jealous of me, but I decide to enjoy that later. "I wish you would have told me," I say quietly.

Cher lets out an exasperated sigh. "Ha! What would I have said? 'Hey, Emma, I know you've liked Connor for, like, ever, and now he likes you too, but I also like him, and it's making me jealous and angry, so like, can you stop?'" She rolls her eyes and flops back onto the bed.

Ruby's leaning up against the wall, with her hands folded over her stomach, looking very wise. She shrugs her shoulders.

Cher sits back up, her cheeks pink. "But it was more than that too." Her voice is quiet, meek like I've never heard it before. "You were so busy worrying about Connor that you stopped noticing everything else. I needed you, but you were too oblivious to see it."

"We tried asking you what was going on. You never wanted to talk about it," I say defensively.

"Yeah, I know. But I didn't want to talk about it then. Maybe I would have talked about it the next day. But I'm sure something exciting happened with Connor, so..." She trails off.

My stomach twists. Maybe I kept choosing a boy over my friends.

"Well, what's going on?" Ruby asks, reaching her hand out to Cher.

Cher grabs it. "I don't know. There's no, like, major news. It's just…" She pauses again and lets go of Ruby's hand to wipe an escaped tear. "Even though it's been over a year, it still sucks that my parents are divorced. Their lives weren't the only ones to change. My life is totally different now too. And sometimes, it hits me when I'm not expecting it, like I'm being punched in the stomach."

Ruby and I are quiet. I know Cher has a hard time with the lives both her parents have now—her dad with his new family, her mom single and dating—but I let myself forget about the new life Cher has, the new life she didn't ask for. I think of Cher crying in the fitting room at the mall the other day. My cheeks flush, and my throat is tight. How could I have been so self-centered?

"I'm not blaming you," Cher says, wiping another silent tear sliding down her cheek. "I'm trying to be honest about how I felt. And maybe I should have done that sooner."

"I'm sorry, Cher." I scoot closer to her on the bed, so I can hold her hand.

"Me too," Ruby says, again grabbing Cher's other hand. "And I totally know that feeling of being punched in the gut. It's like all of a sudden, out of nowhere, I'm so sad or angry, I feel like I could burst. Why did this have to happen to me? Why did *my* dad have to die? Why does *my* life have to be so hard?"

Cher nods, her cheeks splotchy. I reach out for Ruby's hand now, so the three of us form a circle on my bed.

"I'm sorry too. I'm so sorry." Cher's voice cracks on the second sorry. "I'm a horrible friend." She lets go of our hands. "Why did you even invite me here? I wouldn't want to be my friend anymore."

"Because that's what real friendship is," I tell her.

Cher looks down at the kitties on her pants, but this time with a hint of a smile playing on her lips.

Ruby leans back against the wall again. "Yeah. We love you even if you were an asshole. And take you back when you realize the girls you ditched us for are horrible."

"They really are. Ugh," Cher groans. "They spend all of lunch talking crap about everyone else at school."

"No surprise there," Ruby says.

"Well, how about this: Did you know Zoe texts Audrey every morning to see what color underwear she's wearing, so they can match?"

"What?"

"That is really freakin' weird."

"I know!" Cher exclaims with the first real smile I've seen from her all night.

"We will not be doing that," Ruby says.

Cher leans forward and reaches her arms out. "I missed you guys," she says, wrapping us in a hug.

"We missed you too," I tell her.

"Yeah," Ruby starts, leaning back to look at Cher, "but if you ever ghost us again, I will kick your skinny little booty. If you're upset about something, you have to talk to us about it."

I nod solemnly in agreement.

"And Connor is a doofus. You can both do better than him," Ruby adds. "He tried to touch Emma's boob," she explains to Cher.

Cher whips her head toward me, "What?" Her eyes go briefly to my chest.

"Yeah..." I tell Cher about what happened at the park.

"I wondered why you ran off so fast," Cher says after I'm done. "Connor didn't say anything, and I mean, I didn't ask because, you know, we weren't talking." She pauses. "Are you okay?"

I nod. "I'm fine. I don't like him anymore, obviously."

"Me neither," she announces.

"Oh, thank God," Ruby says, rubbing her temples.

I giggle. "Forget him!"

Ruby breaks into a wide grin. "Forget him!"

Cher closes her eyes and shakes her head, but she's also smiling. Ruby and I continue chanting. I'm bouncing on the bed, and Ruby is doing a little shimmy with her shoulders.

Finally, Cher joins in, "Forget him!" She raises her hands up above her shoulders.

All three of us burst into giggles.

Once we stop laughing, Ruby pulls us into a quick hug. "I'm happy you're back, Cher."

"Me too," she says.

"Me three," I add.

Ruby sits back and drops her hands onto her knees. "Okay. Let's go make some nachos." She climbs over us and hops off the bed. Cher and I laugh and do the same. I hip-bump Cher as we walk toward my bedroom door. She smiles and then follows Ruby. I pause at the top of the stairs, watching my two best friends bound down into the kitchen, shouting about cheese.

"Emma, where's the parmesan?"

"Ruby, we do not need parmesan cheese on nachos."

I guess that even without boobs or a boyfriend, I'm still pretty lucky. I race down the stairs and into the kitchen in time to shout, "No tomatoes!" before Ruby can try to sneak them on.

What's next for Emma? You'll have to wait and see…

To get the inside scoop on future books or projects, head over to **@rebeccagarner_author** on Instagram. If you want to be the first to hear exciting announcements and receive behind-the-scenes sneak peeks, be sure to sign up for my newsletter while you're there.

Acknowledgments

Writing acknowledgments feels like such a daunting task because I want to thank so many people. Through my experience working with the Creator Institute and New Degree Press, I learned that writing and publishing a book is a community effort. I'm so grateful to my community for helping me get here.

Thank you to Professor Eric Koester for the incredible opportunity to be part of the Creator Institute and for reminding us over and over again that great books are RE-written. To Professor Haley Newlin, who was the first person to tell me I was an author. And to my editor, Whitney McGruder, who had to answer too many questions like, "Should I cut this?" or "Should I add this here?" or "Which chapter title do you like better?"

Thank you to my friends and family who have been cheering me on from the start, especially Mary, for always checking in and much-need hugs; Sarah & Brandt, for bringing my number-one fan into the world; MS, for never-ending encouragement and IT support; and The Girlfriends, for Vegas bombs, renditions of "What's Up," and the inspiration for true friendship.

Even bigger thank yous to my parents, Mutti and Vati, who have always supported all of my dreams; my sister, Rachel, who is my biggest cheerleader; my daughter, Lucy, just because I love her; and most of all to my husband, Stephen, who didn't hesitate for a second before telling me, "You should do it," when I floated the idea of publishing my book. I'd like you even if you called it "French kissing."

And finally, thank you to my presale campaign supporters. I truly could not have done this without you. Jane & Fred Garner, Katy Vega, Jennifer Thiel, Lana Madsen, Thomas & Sarah Ciezczak, Kassie Carey, Rachel & John Zawaski, Alyssa & Jeremy Linares, Ashliegh Allen, Julia Kelly, Kristin Rybarczyk, Kayley Ramirez, Caryn Muirhead, Stephen McDermott, Caitlin Flood, Laura Ouellette, Amanda Sullivan, Robert Golden, Eric Koester, Natally Klocek, Katie Burns, Melissa Small, Elizabeth Rapp, Rachel Thome, Lori Lysik, Mary Ellen Weber, Pam Conlon, Eugenia Gavrilos, Anna Mendoza, Laura Nowak, Julia Goralka, Terece Hahn, Patti Golden, Ailish Doherty, Mary Crout, Lisa Banos-Cruz, Jennifer DeWitt, Amanda Ampey, Nivene Judeh, Rachel Craig, Lauren Burns, Alyssa Boecker, Jamie Duggan, Amy Anderson, Katie Kean, Heidi Murphy, Michelle Dyer, Sue Ontiveros, Cathy McDermott, Alyssa Egan, Brianne Baffoe, Patty Hopkins, Lauren Holtz-Davalos, JoAnn Reilly, Rhonda Julliano, Mary Ellen Schiavone, Amanda Butz, Carmen Maria Navarro, Mary Sue Marzullo, Valerie Bragg, Shannon Scott, Marsha Fogarty, Sarah & Brandt Hertenstein, Kara Gallagher, Lauren Bartleson, Haley Wrenn & Stan Bukowski, Zenora Evans, Sarah Sheehan, Tara Fogarty, Mary Schleyer, Lisa Hardie, Jennifer Stanislawski, Ali White, Barb Gorno, Melanie Clark, Kimber Sansone, Lindsay McCool, Suzanne Ostrowski, Sonam Tanna Sidhu, Brittany Hertenstein, Elizabeth Zawaski, Moira OConnor, Jen Welsh, Jessica Larsen, Kevin McCool, Josie Murray, Kim Nolan, Melissa Ryan, Belynn Burruel, David Garner, Maggie Duddleston, Sara Kittinger, Caitlin Yarbro, Ashley Sullivan, Tina Vetrovec, Kaitlyn Simon, Erin Dugan, Regina

Fischer, Justin Petrick, Sarah Murphy, Daniel Klimczak, Lisa Pokorny, Jan Short, Anna Montanari, Laura Anzelmo, Shoshan Washington, Patty Gleason, Kathleen Boecker, Gretchen Vickers, Jacqueline Hays, Rebecca Mejia, Megan Schiavone, Sam Bartell, Jessica Mitterman, Lauren Burke, Laura Gleason, Amanda Bennett, Alyx Kay, Erin Niemeyer, Dylan Adams, Michelle Remmenga, Kevin Fogarty, Jennifer Tam, Catherine Gillen, Shannon Mikkelsen, Ashley Myers, Erin McGuire, Nancy Nelson-Druhan, Katelyn Muirhead, Valerie Zulevic, Cheryl Floramo, Brittany Osipavicius, Shannon Bennett, Haley Newlin, Roxanne Adams, Nancy Dubetz, Dasom Lee, Rita Sparks, Meg Reppen, Stephanie Calhoun, Michael Vari, Jennifer Harmening, Alyssa Smith, Nora McMahon, Deanna Santman, Tiffany Wring, Jessica Fuller, Joe Fogarty, Alex Johnston, Missy Zagorski, Kimberly Garner, Linda Sellers, Stephanie Melendez, Fidelma O'Rourke, Sara Hertenstein, Lauren DiTullio, Amy Guzman, Tanya Taylor, Valerie Plocharczyk, Kerry Ewert, Wendy Aviles, Alisha Wielfaert, Amy Kish, Katherine Dolan, Deanna Gaines, Kimberly Marshall, Stefanie Hanyzewski, Kristen Miller, Melissa Kurtz, Darlene Barton, Vickie Adams, Paul Ruppert, Renee Ridolfi, Jessica Burgwald, Brittany Hennigan, Julie Janin, Kristyn Lyerly, Brighid Burns, Lindsey Redd, Katie Wulff, Kimberly Royal, Janelle Svozil, Liam Dolan, Elizabeth Worley, Chrissy Olson, Angela Ingrassia, Amy Mott, Emily White, Maureen Filippini, Jean Telander, Carly Gallagher, Jessica Greene, Carly Melone, Julia Boecker, Nicole Lesh, Emily McCormick, Amber Hamilton, Aurora Melnyk, Samantha DiLallo, Colleen Kempton, Ashley Angone, Kristine Soto, Alexandra Chamoff, Lisa Beck, Matthew Clifford, Kelly Vandenberg, Linda Blaeser, Michael Richards, Erika Vanwitzenburg, Ann Lang, Rebecca Behnke, Kelly Arndt, RoseMarie Benson, Shelly West, and Alec Sander.